CLAIMING HER ALIEN WARRIOR

2

MINA CARTER

NEW YORK TIMES & USA TODAY BESTSELLING AUTHOR

CONTENTS

1

---

*L*ittle green men weren't so little.

Or green.

A member of the Terran Military Defense Force all her life, Major Jane Allen had expected to be involved in a first contact situation at some point. She hadn't, however, expected the Lathar. Somehow, she doubted that *anyone* expected the Lathar.

They were less little green men and more large, ripped, scarily-attractive alpha male warriors hot enough to make any red-blooded woman weak at the knees. Even one mid-divorcee, who'd sworn off men, of any species, for life, like her. She had to admit, they were nice to look at. Considering she was a guest on the Latharian home world, it was a good thing she found them appealing.

"No, Your Majesty. *One,* two, three...*one,* two, three...that's it. Perfect."

Jane looked across the room. Kenna, formerly a Marine under her command, and now one of the four women visiting the Latharian home world, was teaching the emperor, Daaynal, how to waltz. Jane's lips twisted into a small smile.

Like most of the Lathar, Daaynal wore leather armor and heavy combat boots. With the warrior's braids in his long hair, and a face that could have coined the phrase "wickedly handsome" he made an odd sight with Kenna in his arms. Especially as she wore the flowing skirts traditional for Latharian women but with a blaster strapped to her waist.

She and Kenna were living proof you could take the girl out of the Marines, but never the marine out of the girl.

Daaynal was a quick study, his hold and steps perfect within minutes to spin and twirl Kenna around the room. A large room, it was part of the emperor's personal chambers and grandly decorated. Jane lay on a luxurious couch, full after the excellent food at lunch and watched the dance lesson.

Daaynal, she'd decided within minutes of meeting him, was a delight. Handsome, charming... and ruthless. No one kept such a high position in a warrior society where assassination was a viable promotional tactic unless they would do whatever it took to stay there.

He might have Kenna and Cat enthralled, but Jane had seen enough of his type during her long career to have her head turned by a pretty face and hot body. As if to prove her point, Daaynal caught her looking at him as they turned in front of her couch and winked.

She grinned and winked back. He knew what she knew about him and didn't care. He also thought he had her worked out.

Oh no, handsome. We're just getting started.

Talking of good-looking faces, it was almost time for her comm call with her liaison at Terran Command. The highlight of her day. Not. Myles Fuller was not her favorite person. He was too cookie-cutter career track officer for her liking. One who had his eye on a political career and using military service to pad his resume. A service record always looked good on the campaign trail. Plus he had a father with enough brass on his collar to make sure little Myles was in no danger of ever setting foot on a battlefield.

Good. Because he was the sort of rich, entitled asshole playing soldiers she fucking hated. The sort who'd hole up safe in their offices during the colony wars while real soldiers did the dying. Soldiers like her brother, who'd never returned.

Sighing, she levered herself off the couch.

"With your permission, Your Majesty, I have a prior appointment to attend to."

"Of course, of course!" Daaynal replied as he and Kenna breezed past. "I look forward to the pleasure of your company at the banquet this evening."

Ugh, more food. She doubted she'd be able to eat another thing this week, but she bowed anyway and backed out the door.

Her boots rang out against the polished floor of the corridor as she headed toward her quarters. As honored guests, the human women had suites near the emperor's rooms. Security into the wing was high, as it should be after the purist attack at Cat and Tarrick's wedding. No one knew when and where they'd strike again, but Daaynal was taking chances with the human women. Jane approved. One thing she'd learned about fanatics during her long career was they were unbalanced as hell and never, ever, gave up.

She sighed and ran a hand through her hair. A close-cropped blond pixie cut, it fascinated the servants. She'd stopped them putting flowers and jewels in it. They'd finally realized she took them out within minutes anyway.

The palace reminded her of old movies about ancient Rome. It was all white columns and gauze drapes. She half expected a bunch of giggling handmaidens in togas to walk by. Instead, a broad-shouldered figure in leather armor rounded the corner.

Recognition hit. Karryl K'Vass.

Suppressing the quiver of awareness deep in her stomach, she kept walking. Karryl was one of the warriors who'd attacked and boarded the base she'd been stationed at, Sentinel Five. Even though she and the rest of the personnel aboard had put up a good fight, superior weaponry had won the day and the Lathar had taken them all prisoner. Not before she'd given them a damn good run for their money though. She and her unit had holed up in the central section of the base and made a right nuisance of themselves to the invaders.

Then... Karryl had happened.

She studied the warrior walking toward them. Taller than most Lathar, he was well-muscled with inky-black hair she itched to run her hands through. He had beautiful turquoise and violet eyes that should have looked out of place on such a strong face, but suited him to perfection. His battered leather armor fit him like a second skin, its only ornamentation the broad dull-gold sash across his chest. It marked him as something similar to a security officer.

A security officer with a face like thunder.

Uh oh.

He marched up to her, stopping barely a foot from her to loom dangerously. The moment they'd met, the big Lathar had tried to lay claim to her. Tried and failed. Since then he'd tipped between charming in an effort to get her to accept his claim, and frustration when she wouldn't. From his dark expression, looked like today was the latter.

"Why didn't you tell me you had a mate?"

MAJOR JANE ALLEN, warrioress from Earth, was the bane of Karryl's life.

Slender and lithe, she had cropped light hair an

almost white color he'd never seen before but it was her eyes that mesmerized and frustrated him in equal measures. Different colors, one blue and one green, they met his gaze head on with a firm expression and steely disposition he'd struggle to find in many warriors.

He waited for a second and there it was, the slight uplift of her left eyebrow that either showed curiosity, or she thought he was a freaking idiot. He had no idea half the time which it was. Probably both.

"Why didn't I tell you I had a mate?" Her voice was low and melodious, with a pleasing timbre that stroked along his senses like a caress. "Perhaps because I don't?"

He bit back a sigh of frustration.

"Your base records say otherwise. They say you are mated to an Admiral Scott Johnson."

He almost snarled the words. Fury surged through him at the thought of the slender female in another man's arms. *His* woman. He'd wanted her from the moment he'd seen her, crouched behind a makeshift barricade on the base, bellowing orders as she and her men fought the Lathar boarding parties.

Not expecting women on the human base at first, he'd thought the higher-voiced, slender-figured warrior was a youth. Her face shielded by a cap, her body armor had hidden any hint of her female figure. The battle had raged back and forth. He'd been impressed with the youth's training and command over his men. It wasn't until she'd removed the cap he realized his opponent was female. Their gazes met across the battlefield and he'd known. This woman was his, sent by the ancestor gods to be the other half of his soul.

His own little warrioress.

He fought the urge to shake his head. That any society with fertile females would send them into battle was incomprehensible to him. Females were to be pampered and protected, cosseted and looked after... Not allowed to put themselves in harm's way.

But as much as he tried, Jane resisted all his attempts to pamper or protect her. She seemed to delight in thwarting his efforts to claim her, as though she found them, and him, amusing.

"They do, do they?" She folded her arms over her chest and the movement pulled the fabric of her tunic tight across her breasts.

He tried to ignore it, really he did, keeping his eyes level on hers, but the effort cost him. Unlike the other human women, Jane had not adopted the flowing robes of a Latharian woman. Instead, she wore an earth top that bared her arms, tucked into a pair of reenaas combat pants, the hardy material conforming to her curves in a way that made his mouth water. Combat boots and a heavy blaster pistol on her hip completed the picture.

His jaw ached and he half lifted a hand to rub at it as he remembered just how fast she could move, and what one of those boots felt like jammed under his chin.

"Yes, they do."

He folded his arms to match her posture. She was shorter than he was so he had to look down at her to glare, but he wasn't under any illusion he had the upper hand. Sure, he was bigger and stronger, but she was fast and mean as a liras snake. If she'd been male, she'd have made the perfect warrior.

Humans didn't call themselves warriors. They used words like *soldier* and *marine* instead. It all amounted to the same. From what he could work out, Jane was a famous warrior on her home planet. The standard to which all female warriors aspired to, probably half the men as well.

"Well, I guess we still are then." She shrugged. "At least until I sign the divorce papers. I was going to, but then these asshole aliens blew holes in my base."

Her words rocked Karryl. He'd been expecting a denial, some story about records error... that she had never accepted this Admiral Johnson's claim over her... Not a calm confirmation she was, in fact, mated. Which meant, under the terms of the fledgling agreements between their peoples, she could leave Lathar and return to Earth any time she chose.

Unlike an unmated woman, she didn't have to consider any warrior's claim. Even his.

For a week she'd dodged his attempts to claim her. He'd made no pretense of his interest. He'd played nice, been polite, tried to understand her culture was different from his... All the time she'd known she could just laugh and walk away.

"No," he snarled as rage clouded his mind. "Not his. Mine."

Reaching out a hand, he cupped the back of her neck and hauled her up against him. She hit his chest with a gasp, her eyes wide. Good. Finally, he'd surprised her.

"Karr—"

He didn't let her finish, crushing her mouth beneath his. The first taste of her lips almost unmanned him. She might have been forged in the fires of combat, her body all lean lines and toned muscles, but her lips were a different story.

Soft under his, they were as delicate as a *quuarrian* fruit. She'd frozen, hands on his broad chest and he braced himself for a hard knee to the groin. She was not a woman to let an assault on her person go unpunished.

Determined to experience as much as he could before she pushed him away, he moved his lips over hers. Tasting, exploring... needing. Desperate. He needed to remember this. Imprint what it felt like to hold her in his arms, to feel her soft lips under his. Because she would push him away, he knew she would. If she found him suitable as a mate, then she'd have already accepted his claim.

Her lips parted on a soft moan and offered him a glimpse of the seven heavens. Stunned for a second, he didn't move, then all his male instincts roared into life. With a growl, he tilted his head and plundered her lips. The warmth and sweetness of her mouth almost brought him to his knees.

Sliding his tongue against hers, he sought her flavors. The sweet fruits and wine they'd dined on for lunch combined with something else... something haunting and unique. Within a heartbeat he knew one kiss would never be enough. He could kiss her for this lifetime and the next, but it still wouldn't suffice. With one kiss, she'd made him an addict, seeking that next hit until the day he died.

"No..." She snatched her lips from his with a gasp, looking up at him with wide, dark eyes. For a moment, he saw desire and need before her expression shuttered again. "No. We can't."

"What?" His demand was barked as he gripped her upper arms. She'd surrendered to him, he'd felt it, but now she was saying no?

She looked away, trying to wriggle free of his hold and her cheeks turned bright pink. Since he'd met her, she'd been captured, held prisoner, fought her way out of an enemy ship and almost killed by purists and never once had he seen her bat an eyelid. But now she looked rattled. By him. By what they'd shared.

"You prefer women."

It was the only explanation that made sense. Her brow furrowed as her gaze snapped to his. "What? Don't be ridiculous. I was married to a man. I like men plenty enough."

"Then what?" he demanded, shaking her a little by her upper arms as his anger got the better of him.

Her eyes shimmered with something, but the

expression disappeared before he could analyze it. "Have you ever thought I might not be into *you?*"

OH CRAP, she shouldn't have said that.

Jane leaned against the door inside her quarters and took a fortifying breath. The stunned, then hurt, then furious look on Karryl's face when she'd lied and told him she didn't like him had cut her to the quick. She *did* like him, way too much for comfort. That was the problem.

Well, no, that wasn't the real problem. The real issue was she had morals. And she was a spy. She wouldn't, *couldn't*, use Karryl's feelings against him like that.

The soft *ping-ping-ping* of the comm center in the corner of the room called for her attention. She sighed. Time for her scheduled call with Terran Command. She had to report in every day to let them know more about the alien culture she was immersed in.

What they really wanted to know was how to defeat the Lathar.

Heart heavy, she walked across the room and slid into the seat in front of the console. A touch on the screen activated it. Myles smiling face filled the screen. She smiled a false smile. If the guy were in the room, she'd break his fucking nose.

"Greetings, Major Allen. How are we today?" he asked, rubbing his ear. "I hope you and your lovely companions are having a pleasant break on Lathar Prime."

His words were in code, a predefined speech pattern and set of phrases all high-level command officers knew by heart for just such instances as these. *Translation: Sit-rep.*

"Doing well, thank you, Colonel. And yourself? How's your lovely wife?" Her words followed the same protocol as she flicked her gaze to the top right corner of the screen. *No change. Nothing to report.*

She didn't have anything past the information she had already given them. As charming as the Lathar were, they were careful to keep guests out of sensitive areas. So far, she hadn't been able to gather any information on military numbers or weapons capability.

Myles's expression darkened for a second. "Oh, I'm afraid she's not been well..." *Information required urgently.* Yes, asshole, she knew that. "So she's taken a short break to my uncle's cabin near the lake." *Defense perimeter on high alert.* "If she doesn't get better soon though, I'm insisting she go to St. Michaels."

Shit. Ever the professional, she kept a straight face at the last line. The Terran defense perimeter, comprised of bases and automated defense satellites, worked on a series of named levels. On a normal day the alert was low, at level George, but it went up through Jeremy, Roxanne (she'd love to know who got that one in) and up to Michael. If the defense net was that high, it meant the president had authorized nukes.

"Are you sure that's a good idea?" she frowned. *Stand down, I got this.* "I've always found Dr. Roxanne at All Angels to be an excellent doctor."

Myles rubbed at his chin. "You think? We'll see how she rallies in the next few days. If she doesn't come through then, I'm going to take her to St. Michaels."

She nodded. "Understood. Please pass on my regards to her."

They weren't going to let this go, so the clock ticked. Find out something they could use, or they were arming nukes. And if they fired nukes at the Lathar, long-lost genetic relations or not, humanity was fucking toast.

"Of course, Terran Command out."

She sat for a moment and closed her eyes as tiredness washed over her. President Halland had always been an asshole, but she couldn't believe he'd be stupid enough to arm the nukes. It shouldn't have surprised her. Once a person gained enough power, they seemed to stop listening to common sense and believed whatever their yes-men told them. After his mismanagement of colony farming resources, Halland would never be re-elected so a war was his best bet for retaining power.

With a sigh, she stood and brushed nonexistent lint from her pants and headed for the door. Damned if she did, damned if she didn't, but to prevent an all-out war, she needed to find something to give to Myles.

2

The emperor had summoned him. A private audience.

Pride filled Karryl's chest as he strode along the corridor heading for the Imperial War room. He'd never been summoned personally. He'd only seen the emperor as part of a group under Tarrick's command. He'd be surprised if Daaynal had even known his name before the fight in the courtyard with the R'Zaa, so it was a sign of his growing standing in the court. First Daaynal had publicly declared him a kinsman and now this?

He entered the war room to find it empty. Face set in implacable lines, he scanned the large room, taking in the massive holo-table and the arching windows that gave a view of blue skies overhead.

They didn't show the real sky. Buried beneath the palace, the war room was an impenetrable bunker the emperor could direct his armies from. The windows gave the place a little light, and as the holo display from the table could be extended; they served a functional purpose as well. With one command, the emperor could see the view from any Lathar ship or installation.

A warrior at the far end of the room stepped forward from a shadowed alcove and cleared this throat. Karryl's attention snapped to him. Unlike the other guards in the palace, he wore the insignia of the emperor's own guard.

"This way, *deshenal*," he said with a small bow, pointing to the door behind him. "His Majesty is waiting for you in his inner office."

Deshenal. Honored warrior. It was an old term, not used lightly or without the emperor's command. Karryl couldn't help his chest puffing out with yet more pride as he walked across the room toward the door. He was a male on the up and up, with a good reputation and the favor of the emperor himself.

Anger and frustration rolled through him in equal measure, tightening the muscles in his shoulders and neck as he clenched his hands into fists. Why couldn't Jane see he'd make a good mate?

That he had the standing and power to protect and nurture her?

"Have you ever thought I might not be into you?"

The words slammed through his memory, cutting him to the soul. His boots stomped onto the carpet in the short corridor behind the war room as though they were waging war on the plush pile. Perhaps he should look at other earth women... Palace gossip had it that Daaynal planned to send a diplomatic mission to the human's home planet. There were plenty of women there, and from what the most talkative of the human women, Kenna, had said, many human women would jump at the chance to be a warrior's mate.

The door at the end of the corridor opened. He walked through, a little surprised there was no guard. As soon as he entered the small room he understood why.

Daaynal was not alone. The Emperor's Champion, Xaandril, leaned in front of a console, his big, scarred hands against the smooth surface as he glared at the screen in front of him. A tall, powerfully-built warrior, he was both Daaynal's champion and the man's shadow. Where the emperor went, so did Xaandril.

"It has to be a code," his voice was deep and full

of gravel. He flicked a glance up and speared Karryl with a direct look that made him shiver. "Welcome, K'Vass. Come in, don't lurk in the shadows."

Karryl stepped forward, not wanting to be seen as lurking like a coward or to anger Xaandril. When he was a kid, he'd been brought up on stories of the great war hero, Xaandril. He was a war General. A hero of the Battle of the Nine Wastes, where the Lathar defeated the *Ovverta,* a barbaric race who slaughtered other races for fun.

They'd been the biggest threat the Lathar had ever faced. Now they were all but extinct thanks to Xaandril. Since the man had lost his mate and young daughter to an *Ovverta* attack, Karryl didn't blame the man for his bloodthirstiness where the vile creatures were concerned.

"Thank you, my lord." Karryl inclined his head to Xaandril, then turned his attention to Daaynal and added a small bow. "You wished for my presence, Your Majesty?"

"Indeed." Unlike earlier in the day when he'd hosted a lunch for their human guests, Daaynal was not smiling. He pointed to the screens the two senior Lathar were looking at. "Watch. This may be of interest to you."

Xaandril turned the screens so they could all see,

and Karryl stilled. An image of Jane was frozen on the screen, her face set in what he could tell was a false smile. A flick of Xaandril's fingers and the holo-screen expanded to show a human male in a uniform. It was different than the one Jane or the men on the base had worn, with more fancy bits. It had to be a dress uniform since it would be useless in battle for anything other than making its wearer a prime target.

"The human woman, Jane Allen's, call back home," Daaynal said.

"You're spying on her?" Karryl hid his surprise behind a bland expression. They had to have hidden cameras in her quarters. He knew enough about her to know that if she'd found them, she'd be as mad as a *draanth* and have destroyed them already.

Daaynal inclined his head. "Indeed. It seems our beautiful little human warrior is keeping secrets."

Anger burst through him with the force of an energy blast. *His* warrior, not Daaynals, not anyone else's. His alone. He fought the blaze of fury and the need to introduce Daaynal's face to the console several times. He was a good warrior, fast and merciless in battle, but he was under no illusions. A physical attack on the emperor would end with him getting his ass handed to him on a plate and a prolonged stay in the med bay before his execution. If Daaynal was feeling charitable. If he weren't, then Karryl would die right here in this room. Slowly and painfully.

It answered a question though. The reaction to the thought of someone else claiming Jane as theirs meant he wouldn't be looking for another female on earth. He didn't want another female. He wanted this one. Her.

He looked at the screen again, studying the male. His rage simmered within. Was this her mate? Was that who she called when she excused herself to "report to Terran Command"? The male was smooth-skinned and plastic-looking, smaller in stature than any Lathar. He didn't look like he'd ever seen a battlefield in his life. She preferred that?

"Who is he?" He kept his voice level with supreme effort. All he wanted to do was reach through the screen and smack the ever-loving *draanth* out of the guy.

"A Commodore Myles Fuller."

Karryl let go a sigh of relief. Not Admiral Scott Johnson then. This wasn't her old mate. Good, he wouldn't have to track this one down and remove his spinal column from his body.

"See here and here?" Xaandril activated the

recording, pointing out two time stamps. They stood in silence listening to the two humans talking. It seemed to be a harmless conversation about Fuller's wife.

"She sounds normal, other than a little stilted. Have you considered she might not like this Fuller?"

Xaandril shook his head. "It's more than that. I ran their conversation through several algorithms against the databases your war group recovered from their base and two words stand out: Roxanne and Michael."

Karryl shrugged. "What do they mean?"

Daaynal folded his arms, feet spread in a classic at ease posture. "They're names, but they're also part of the human defense system. The names of alert levels. From what we can work out, the humans have armed their crude nuclear capabilities. Which, as I'm sure you're aware, is considered an act of war by intergalactic convention."

"Shit."

Everything within Karryl went stone cold. If that's what the humans had done, then they were fucked. By all the laws of the combined species within the galaxies, just arming "dirty" ordnance like nuclear weaponry was cause to wipe a planet out. They didn't even need to get close to do it. A terraforming warhead from deep space would destroy anything on the planet's surface, wiping the slate clean, then forces could swoop in and pick off any colonies or space stations.

"She appears to be arguing against it," Xaandril mused, rubbing his chin. "So perhaps her punishment should be less severe..."

Daaynal nodded. "Agreed, maybe five lashes of the energy whip instead—"

"Wait, what?" The words escaped Karryl's lips before he could stop them. "We're considering punishing a *female?* A fertile female from a genetically compatible species? For what? For arguing against her superior officer arming nuclear weaponry?"

Both warriors looked at him. It was like being stared at by two *keelaas* snakes. Large enough to swallow a man whole, and with a necrotic bite, they were as scary as hell.

"He seems to want something from her. The only thing she can give them is information. On us. She's spying for them." Daaynal's voice was level, but Karryl got the feeling this was a test. That his reactions now would change things.

"Then we feed her misinformation."

Crap that sounded like he was giving the

emperor himself orders. It was too late to back out now. He had to follow through. "We create a situation with the promise of what she needs, then feed her *draanth* shit."

Daaynal's face split into a broad smile and he looked at Xaandril in triumph. "You owe me ten *lindari,* old man. I told you he'd protect his woman *and* have a sensible idea."

Xaandril grumbled and dug in his pocket for a credit slip. He slapped it into Daaynal's hand. Karryl blinked in surprise. He didn't know what shocked him more; the fact the two most senior warriors in the empire were betting for small change, or that the emperor had bet on *him.*

"Okay, down to business." Daaynal flicked out a chair and shoved it on its rollers toward Karryl. "We need to work out how to tempt your little human warrior."

THE LATHAR WERE A CONTRARY RACE. All war-like one moment, then the next they took a pleasant afternoon ride into the countryside like they were in some Regency novel.

"This is lovely, isn't it? I love the colors of the

flowers they have here," Cat commented. The four women were safely tucked into a carriage rather than given mounts. Kenna had argued, as usual, saying she was a more than competent equestrian back on earth and that the horses had six legs rather than four was no problem.

Jane hadn't argued. She'd never been the horsey type anyway, and the fact the monsters the Lathar rode had teeth like vampires' and claws to boot, meant she wasn't likely to change her mind soon. At all. Ever.

The trouble was, how the hell was she going to get any intel from a carriage?

"The flowers are pretty," she replied, sitting up in her seat to look ahead. They were traveling faster than she'd thought possible and the horse-creatures' six-legged gait was almost beautiful. She'd had to look down to make sure they didn't have wings on their feet or something as strange, but no, they ran just like earth horses, only a lot faster.

"Looks like we're slowing down."

The warriors around them tightened their reins, pulling their steeds to a trot then a walk at the top of a rise. Jane looked around and couldn't help sucking in a breath as the carriage pulled to a stop. The alien countryside lay beneath them, a jade and turquoise masterpiece. A swathe of golden-leaved trees cut an arc across the landscape with the white splendor of the distant palace like the jewel in a crown.

"It's beautiful," she breathed, her mission forgotten for the moment. How many humans had seen something like this... The sheer beauty of an alien planet. She'd been on other planets before, but the colonies weren't anything like this. They were dull, drab places full of broken-down people desperate for a better life than being crammed into slums back on earth. Only the wealthy got to live in places like this with open skies and vegetation.

"I'm glad you approve of my home."

A deep voice beside her made her turn in surprise to find Karryl at the side of the carriage. He extended a hand to help her down and the side stair slid down to allow her to step out. Putting her hand in his larger one, she suppressed her shiver at the latent strength she felt.

He was a large man, strong and so gentle at the same time that she didn't know how to react to him most of the time. But something was different, his easy smile the same, but the expression in his eyes guarded and shuttered.

Shit. She'd hurt him when she'd said she wasn't into him.

Pausing on a step, she looked him in the eye. "Karryl, I apologize for what I said earlier. I didn't mean the insult or to be cruel."

He shrugged. "Think nothing of it. Can I persuade you to accept my company for the afternoon?"

"Of course, I'd be delighted."

Taking the rest of the steps more delicately than her heavy boots and combat pants would suggest, she smiled up at him. "Your planet is lovely. Did you grow up here?"

"I did. On a small estate to the north. It's a lot colder than it is here but with mountains so high you can't see the tops."

The other warriors and their mounts milled around them. Taking her arm, he used his body to shield her from the snorting, stamping creatures, and led her onto the grass where blankets had been laid.

"Really?" she smiled, glad to have found common ground. He ushered her to one of the blankets to take a seat. A quick glance behind her confirmed the other women were well looked after. "I love the mountains at home. My father used to take us rock climbing in the summer. Do you have any pictures?"

He shook his head, his inky-black hair dancing on his shoulders. "Not with me. I have one in my qua —" A strange expression crossed his face. "I'll find it and bring it to the banquet tonight for you."

She sat back, her arms wrapped around her knees. Karryl stretched out next to her, leaning on one elbow, more relaxed than she'd ever seen him. For a moment, like almost every conversation they'd had, she'd been sure he would try and get her into his rooms. He hadn't. Proof of just how much she'd damaged things between them with her words.

She needed him. Guilt made her stomach churn. Crap. She'd never thought she would be this kind of person. A user. Even though she knew how he felt about her, that he wanted to claim her as his mate... He was her best hope of getting the information she needed.

"Okay, I'd like that." Not wanting to overplay her hand, she slid him a sideways smile and concentrated on the scenery. Silence fell between them and she kicked herself. Oh great, what the hell did she say now? Looking around her, she tried to find inspiration. There was always the weather, but she was so not going there. She couldn't be *that* bad at conversation...surely?

Three painful, silent minutes later, she had to

admit she was. And it was no surprise. She'd been in the military since eighteen, so dates had been few and far between. Quick shags when off-duty? Sure, she'd had plenty. They hadn't needed much in the way of flirtation and talking. Then she'd met Scott. Three months later they were married, again with the minimum of talking or flirtation.

She wrinkled her nose as she thought back. They'd had, what... six in-depth conversations in their entire marriage? During the time they'd been "together" anyway. They separated after a year but remained married for...well, until now. She still had to sign the papers...the only reason that Karryl hadn't pressed his claim against her.

"Do you think it would be possible to get my personal belongings sent from the base?" she asked.

He turned his head to look at her and she was caught by his unusual gaze. She'd never tire of looking at his eyes. They were jewel-like with multiple colors and slitted.

"Your eyes are similar to a cat's I once had." Great, now she was babbling. "His pupils went round like that. Usually when indoors. Why do yours?"

He lifted one eyebrow, and then his lips quirked. An actual expression rather than the polite mask he had been giving her. "You mean pupil dilation? What does it mean for humans?"

"Hmm..." She nibbled her lower lip. "Either being in a darkened environment so the eye can gather more light. We don't see well in the dark, though, something about the way our eyes are constructed."

"Or?"

She frowned. "Or what?"

He watched her. "You said 'either' but gave one choice. What is the second?"

"Oh." She couldn't do anything about the blush that hit her cheeks at light speed. "It means attraction. Sexual attraction and to attract a member of the opposite gender."

His smile widened a little. "There you go then."

She blinked. "It means the same for Lathar? Well, the eye rounding thing?"

His nod was distracted by a commotion on the other side of the group. Several warriors sprang to their feet, weapons appearing from nowhere.

"Is there a problem?" the emperor called out, levering himself to his feet from the rug he'd been sitting on near Tarrick and Cat. His face was wreathed in frowns.

"A rider, Your Majesty," a guard replied,

binoculars to look through. "Approaching at speed. He's... yes, he's wearing imperial colors. One of your personal guard."

"Interesting." Daaynal stood to the side of the guard and held out his hand for the binoculars.

Jane, sensing the tension in the group, rose when Karryl did. His expression was implacable, but she could feel the coiled strength in his body. Ready for action at a moment's notice. His hand hovered over the blaster at his hip and she envied him being armed. This was a bad location for cover. An air strike would take them all out in one go.

"Ahh, it's Caayan. I know him." The tension in the air disappeared at the words. "It has to be something important if he's ridden out. Let him through."

The rider, Caayan, reached them within minutes and the outer circle of warriors parted to let him ride right in. He brought the snarling, stamping creature to a stop just before Daaynal. The beast snarled at him, but the emperor smiled and rubbed the animal's nose.

"Caayan, you bring news?" he asked as the rider jumped to the ground and bowed low.

"Indeed, Your Majesty." The warrior's expression was careful, but even Jane could see the concern lurking behind the polite mask. "We've received word the facility at *L'Raanis Three* has been compromised. There's been no communication since early this morning and the drone we sent on a flyby was rendered inoperative by unknown forces."

Jane's ears picked up. Caayan had kept his voice down, but she had excellent hearing. What facility was *L'Raanis Three*? As far as she'd been able to work out, the Lathar infrastructure was comprised of the war group ships. She hadn't been able to find any information on orbital or deep space communications arrays anywhere, but they had to have them. This sounded like it could be it.

Daaynal sighed, shaking his head. "If L-three goes down, then we'll lose contact with the war groups in the *Rivaas* Sector. We can't afford that."

Yes! Jane almost punched the air. She'd been right, it *was* a communications array. And she'd found that out without using Karryl.

The emperor looked up and around, spotting the two of them. He motioned Karryl over. "Karryl, my kinsman. Attend me."

"Stay here," he murmured, sliding his hand down her arm in a brief, and unexpected caress. Surprised, she did as ordered, watching him cross to Daaynal. She realized her mouth was open like a damn guppy, so she snapped it shut as the small group of Lathar huddled and spoke in lowered voices she couldn't hear.

It didn't matter. If Karryl was going to this L-three facility, then so was she. Whatever it took.

3

"*I*'m thinking a purist attack." Daaynal kept his voice low, so the group around them didn't hear.

Karryl didn't blame him, a hill in the middle of the countryside was not the best place to be discussing a potential threat to the empire, but he wasn't going to argue. This was the second time the emperor had called on him, and the second time Daaynal had called him kinsman. Always before, he would have been one of the warriors guarding the perimeter, not one of the chosen few. But that didn't mean he was going to keep his mouth shut and play the yes-man. It just wasn't in his nature.

"Divide and conquer?" He folded his arms and considered other warriors. Tarrick had joined them, his mate Cat gathering the human women and keeping them safely within the center of the ring of guards.

Daaynal nodded. "The war groups currently in that sector have known purist leanings. Isolation would leave them ripe for infiltration."

Shit. Yeah, it would. He'd been thinking more outright attack, but warriors without a clan often attached themselves to others. A sharp charlatan could have some of the less intelligent males dancing to their tune quickly. From there it was a quick hop to a coup and taking over the clan. If that happened with enough war groups... It would be a disaster. All-out war in the empire.

"That's..." Tarrick curled his lip, "dishonorable."

Daaynal shrugged. "We're not dealing with men who have honor. I want intel and fast, and the group of warriors I trust is small and select. I do not want anything to threaten this alliance with the humans."

Unless the humans threatened it themselves, of course. Karryl kept his thoughts and their previous conversation to himself, not sure if Daaynal had confided in Tarrick or not. He probably had. It was no secret at court that Daaynal wouldn't allow his nephews to roam the galaxy forever. Take Laarn, for example, any moment now the court expected an announcement that he had been confirmed as Lord Healer. Tarrick would suffer a similar "fate." Karryl's money was on Imperial Viceroy, so much so he had a book running with the other warriors in the war group.

One thing none of them would bet on was who would take over the K'Vass on Tarrick's promotion. Karryl and Jassyn were of equal rank and status, it could be either... Karryl intended it to be him.

Daaynal carried on talking. "Okay, Tarrick. You will return to Earth space and strengthen our position there. I assume Fenriis has now arrived, that will give you two full war groups to hold the sector. You will need to handle negotiations in my name, which will be good practice."

Karryl hid his smile as Tarrick blinked in shock. "Good practice for what?"

Daaynal merely waved his hand, apparently not in the mood to answer, and speared Karryl with a look.

"Karryl, you will take one of my combat flyers and investigate the situation at *L'Raanis Three.*"

"Of course, Your Majesty." He inclined his head in respect, then looked up. "Regards to my ... previous task?"

The emperor shrugged. "Inconsequential for

now; this takes precedence. You'll leave as soon as possible after we return to the palace."

Turning, he raised his voice. "Change of plans. Playtime is over, pack up everything."

It took mere minutes for the blankets to be packed and the group on their way back. Deliberately, Karryl didn't look at Jane as they set out. She called his name when he'd mounted his *kervasi* but he picked a position at the front of the group instead.

"Trouble in paradise?" Tarrick asked, drawing his mount level.

Karryl lifted an eyebrow. "Another Earth phrase, my lord? You'll be totally converted soon."

"You *draanthic!*" Tarrick chuckled, shaking his head, but despite his amusement, Karryl knew he wasn't going to get away without answering the question. Tarrick had *that* look in his eye, one all his warriors knew. And sure enough, his next question was straight to the point. "So...you've decided to give up pursuit of the lovely earth major?"

He reined in a little, knowing the carriage was coming up behind them. Open-topped, it would be easy for the occupants to hear everything he and Tarrick said. Good. Payback time.

"A warrior can only beat his head against a

bulkhead so long before brain damage occurs." He shrugged. "The hopes that I harbored my claim would be welcomed have been relegated to daydream and fantasy. Perhaps another human female will find my advances acceptable, should I get the chance to return to that area of space."

Tarrick's expression shifted, and he nodded. The barest flicker of his gaze toward the carriage told Karryl he read between the lines.

"Perhaps that is the wisest course. These earth women are unpredictable and prone to decisions that make no sense to us. Perhaps the differences in our cultures are a little too wide."

"Indeed, indeed. At present, though, I don't have the time to study another culture to make myself more amenable to a mate. I have duties to fulfill."

"Of course. Totally understandable."

They topped a rise to find the palace laid out below them and came to a stop as the carriage got a wheel stuck in a rut. Karryl took a moment to gaze on the palace. He couldn't help a small sigh of contentment. He'd always loved the place. Its peace and tranquility, its sense of history and grandeur. It reminded him of an old Imperial lady, content in the sunset of her life.

"In case I don't see you before you leave on your

new mission..." Tarrick reached out an arm, palm up. A warrior's handshake, between equals. "Go with honor. Do the K'Vass proud."

It was an honor Karryl hadn't expected, the third in a day of complete surprises. It seemed his misfortune in love became fortune to the rest of his life.

He grasped Tarrick's arm with a broad smile. "I intend to, my lord. I intend to."

"Karryl! Karryl, wait!" Jane called out after the swiftly disappearing figure of the Latharian warrior.

She'd jumped out of the carriage almost before it had stopped, almost trampling Kenna in the process. Throwing a quick apology over her shoulder, she set off after her quarry. For a big man, he moved fast, those long, leather-clad legs eating the distance. By the time she reached the door he'd disappeared into from the stable courtyard, he was halfway down the corridor within.

"Karryl, please...would you bloody well hold on!"

He paused near the next corner and looked over

his shoulder. Trotting down the deserted corridor, she reached his side.

"You're leaving?"

No sense in pretending she hadn't heard the conversation that had resulted in them all coming back to the palace, or the exchange with Tarrick. The one that had confirmed her suspicion that her hasty words had ruined things between them.

He inclined his head in reply, a formal gesture that reminded her of an old world vampire from the retro films she'd loved to watch years ago. He'd make an excellent vampire, she realized, with his jewel-like eyes and black hair.

"I am."

"Don't."

The word was out before she could stop it, a plea direct from her soul. She didn't want him to go. Didn't want this whole charade anymore. She wanted things to be simple. To, heaven help her, to have been captured by bloody aliens and not have to play spy for her home world.

"Don't what?" He frowned, turning to her.

Arms folded across his chest, he looked down at her. His lips were a thin line, his expression forbidding, but all she could think about was how his lips felt on hers... about his strong arms around her. Stood as they were, the difference in their sizes, male and female, Lathar and human, was more noticeable. And it thrilled her.

"Don't go."

She was committed now, she might as well go whole hog.

His eyebrow winged up. "Don't go? Did you forget the part about me being a warrior? I go where I am ordered. I would have thought you, of all the earth women, would understand that."

She glared up at him. "Of course, I do, but that's not what I meant."

"Then what did you mean?" he asked, voice a velvet temptation. She caught the little glimmer in his eyes. The bastard was enjoying this.

"Why can't another warrior go? I thought you were assigned to us humans."

He shrugged, a bland expression in place. If he'd have yawned next, it wouldn't have surprised her. Anger surged and she had to resist the temptation to kick him in the shins.

"There are plenty of warriors here to protect you."

A growl of frustration fought to break free of her throat. He *knew* exactly what she was talking about. He was just being difficult. Fucking men.

"You're an asshole."

"*I'm* the asshole?" he barked out a laugh. All amusement dropped from his expression in a nano-second. He moved in a flash. Hard hands closed around her arms and he yanked her against his solid body.

"Have a care, little human, that you don't push me too far." His lips hovered mere-millimeters from hers. His eyes glittered with anger. "I've been willing to look past your ignorance of our culture. I've tried to court you, have let you humiliate me in front of my peers, but never forget I am a man, and a warrior."

Her ability to breathe seemed to have disappeared, her breasts crushed against his broad chest.

"Now, I have a mission. A dangerous one. If you are here when I return, then we will discuss this further."

She started to nod but then found her voice. "Let me come with you."

He shook his head. "It's too dangerous for a female."

His hold relaxed minutely, enough that she could breathe easier, and he slid a hand up to cup the back of her neck. His gaze softened as it moved down to latch onto her lips. Unbidden, they parted in invitation and his eyes darkened in response.

He bent his head and his lips covered hers in a soft kiss that disarmed her. She'd expected him to be rough with anger and demanding, but he wasn't. Instead, he seduced her with soft brushes of his lips against hers, clinging and exploring. She relaxed against him, curling her fingers into the lapels of his uniform jacket.

It was over too soon though, and she murmured in disappointment. Opening her eyes, she found him looking down at her with a small smile on his lips. He reached up and swept a gentle thumb over her lower lip.

"Until I return."

Releasing her, he turned and walked away, not looking back. She wrapped her arms around herself and watched him go.

"Sorry, sweetheart. I'm not prepared to wait that long."

FINDING out which ship Karryl was taking had been child's play. All Jane had to do was follow him when he left his quarters an hour after he'd left her in the corridor. Dressed in the long hooded robes of one of the Oonat servants, she barely warranted a glance from the lathar she passed in the halls as she tailed her mark.

He'd headed for the landing pads visible from the windows of her suite, tucked just behind the emperor's wing of the palace. As a human, she'd never been able to get near the place, but with her face covered and pretending to be one of the Oonat, it was surprisingly easy.

Walking through the last door, she ducked quickly to the side and scooted behind crates rather than walking across the courtyard and through the other archway that led to parts unknown. She hadn't managed to explore this far into the restricted area before.

Karryl's boots rang against the concrete-like surface of the landing pad across from her. Three sleek surface to space shuttles sat in a row on the pad. The boarding hatch was open on the rightmost one, a short flight of steps leading up to it. The big warrior disappeared inside for a moment. When he re-emerged, the large pack over his back was absent. Stowing his gear.

Movements as silent as she could make them, she crept forward. She needed to get inside that shuttle. But how? Despite the fact that it was easily as large as a twenty man troop carrier, she could only see one entrance hatch. Right next to where Karryl stood, a panel on the ship slid back to expose what looked like pipes. Perhaps he was checking the engine or something... she hadn't been able to work out exactly how the Lathar ships were powered. Not conventionally, that was for sure.

Fate played into her hands. With a shake of his head and a frown, he slid the panel back into place and stomped to the back of the ship. Heart in her throat, she took the chance and darted forward. Her boots made no sound on the concrete as she ran across. Every second she expected him to walk back around the ship and spot her, or for someone to enter the courtyard behind her and raise the alarm.

There were no shouts though, and Karryl didn't reappear. She reached the steps without incident and raced up them. Her robes almost caught in the doorway, but she felt the tug and yanked them clear before they tore.

The inside of the craft was more spacious than she'd expected. There were two seats in the cockpit, more like recliners than the upright seats she was used to seeing in human crafts. The rest of the interior was open, an empty space she assumed was multi-functional. Recessed handles in the walls and floor would indicate where furniture unfolded and slid out. Which was all fine and dandy but gave her very few options for concealment.

Hearing heavy boots outside, she bit back her gasp and ran to the back of the cabin. There were three doors in the back wall. On instinct, she opened the smallest one built into the curve of the wall.

Storage boxes and crates met her questing gaze. Bingo. She squeezed into the space and closed the door behind her. Holding her breath, she pressed her ear to the door. Footsteps clunked against the steps. Crap, that had been close. A moment later and he'd have spotted her.

Relief rolling through her, she worked her way to the back of the compartment and wriggled behind a large crate. Unless he actually got in here on his hands and knees, there was no way Karryl would find out she was here.

It was cold, though, and she quickly discovered when the light by the door snapped off, dark. Huddling into a small ball to keep warm, she listened to the noises of the ship around her. There was the *slam-clunk-click* of the outer door as it shut, then a strange whirring which could only be the engines. Frowning, she reached out a hand to the surface beside her to find it vibrating.

The ship lurched and she gasped, reaching out to grab onto the crate but in the next second she was slammed back against the floor and wall. Gritting her teeth, she tried to lift her head but was pinned into place. They were taking off.

She closed her eyes and tried not to think. Unfortunately, her brain hadn't gotten the hint and a small part started to wonder how much more G-force the average lathar could take compared to the more delicate human frame.

Shit, she was about to become space-jam.

4

Karryl was an experienced pilot, but he'd never flown anything quite as luxurious as the personal transport the emperor loaned him. The engines were state-of-the-art, the latest development in hyper-threaded, quad-core faster than light technology. It showed. He barely felt lift off from the planet, the power only detectable when the engines kicked in to slingshot the sleek ship into the planet's outer atmosphere.

Pinned back into the low, padded couch, he kept an eye on the readouts. Well, that's what he told himself. All the screens were within normal parameters, which was good since he wasn't paying attention to them. Thoughts of Jane swirled through his mind, preoccupying his thought processes. He tried to shut them down, put thoughts of the tempting little human out of his head to concentrate on his mission, but the memory of her face when they'd said goodbye kept sneaking in. The image of her eyes, wide and dark, over lips plump from his kisses, tormented him and he groaned.

He didn't have time for this shit. He had a mission. An important one. One that would prove to the emperor he was ready to take on the role of War Commander. He couldn't afford to fuck it up because his brains had been addled by his prick.

The G-forces let up as they reached higher orbit and with a skill belied by the size of his warrior hands, he nudged them around the orbital defenses and into space. A quick course correction later and he engaged the FTL. There was a slight lurch, barely noticeable, and the stars in the view screen became streaks of white.

With a sigh, he released the four-point harness and rolled to a standing position. For a moment, he stood by the pilot's couch, thoughts of Jane filling his head. She hadn't seemed to want him to go. Of course, she was a spy. He'd expressed an interest in her, so he was the soft touch, the one most likely to be open to emotional manipulation. If she thought that, she hadn't learned anything about the Lathar, or him.

The thought of her spying didn't sit well with him. He knew her better than that. She wasn't a spy. She was too open, too honest, a warrior through and through as he was. They'd both been forged on a battlefield, not in the shadows.

With a sigh, he ran a hand through his hair. He didn't want her to be a spy, that was the problem. While he knew she wasn't innocent, he wanted to think of her as honorable.

The same kind of honor that stopped him pressing his claim over her when he really, *really* wanted to. If she turned out to be an underhanded, deceitful *shylakster,* though...he didn't know how he'd react. Severely probably.

Stomping to the middle of the central cabin, he lifted and twisted three catches high on the port side wall, grabbed the handle that protruded from the sleek metal and pulled down the bed. Since this was the emperor's own craft, it wasn't the hard, narrow cot Karryl was used to. Instead, it was a wide, well-padded haven of luxury, complete with cozy *eedireen* blankets.

Not wanting to get such expensive bedding dirty, he sat on the edge of the bed and pulled off his boots. They hit the deck plating with dull thuds. He lay back with a small groan. It felt good to stretch out on a bed where his feet didn't hang over the end. Even for a Lathar, Karryl was tall, almost as tall as Daaynal himself, and most warrior accommodations were built for men at least half a foot smaller.

Closing his eyes, he tried to summon sleep. He should rest. The journey was long and he had no idea what he would find at the other end. If it was worse than he expected or he needed to gather intel, then he may need to stay on his feet for hours...days even, so best to rest now.

As soon as he shut his eyes though, all he saw was his little human warrior. Images of her as she'd fought back when they'd attacked the base, the defiant tilt of her head when they'd finally captured her and her team. Her hard expression on the T'Laat ship when she faced down rival enemy warriors to keep her women safe. Her evasion of each move he made on her until...finally, the memory of her soft lips parted in surrender beneath him.

With a groan, he rolled over and punched the pillow. If he carried on like this, he'd get no sleep. At least, he wouldn't until he took matters in hand... but the last thing he wanted was to have to explain to Daaynal why there was a mess on his beautiful, expensive bedding, so he thought of something safe. Like *draakis* kits, or Xaandril in his underwear. *Eww,* Kaaryl wrinkled his nose. Okay, that was enough to put anyone off.

Closing his eyes again, he let his body relax, deliberately keeping his mind clear so he could drift off. The ship was on autopilot and he was using remote space lanes so there should be no issues between him and his destination. If there were, the computer would wake him. The sheets rustled around him as his limbs went lax and he started to drift into sleep.

Seconds later, the smallest sound from the back of the ship made his eyes snap open. He was alone in the cabin, but his gaze fixed on the small storage door tucked between the wash facilities and the side of the ship. Something moved in there. It couldn't be the cargo settling since it was all crated with mag-grav fastenings. No, it had sounded more like the slide of fabric when someone scooted across the floor on their backside.

Silent and focused, he slid off the bed and padded toward the door. A flick of his wrist dropped a blade into his hand from the sheath on his inner forearm. Light from the strip lights along the top sides of the cabin glittered off the lethal edge. If he had a stowaway, the stupid *draanthic* would regret the day he'd been born. Karryl was in no mood to play nice guy or even semi-not-violent guy.

His lips curled back into a grim snarl as he yanked the door open, reached a hand in and pulled the intruder out. With a spin and a hard shove, he pinned his captive's front side against the door with his bigger body, the knife kissing the skin of her throat.

Wait, what... *Her* throat?

His intruder was small and curvy, wearing the silver-gray robes of an Oonat. His body took that moment to remind him that thanks to his pursuit of Jane, he hadn't been with a female for far too long. After having spent more than five minutes in the company of the human females, the animal-like docility of the oonat disgusted him. His lip curling, he made to push the creature away when her hood slipped to reveal a short crop of silver-blond hair.

"Jane?" Snatching the blade away from her throat, he spun her around so her back hit the wall. "What the hell are you doing here? I almost killed you!"

Oh, shit. Jane met Karryl's angry gaze and tried not to shiver. The big warrior had a face like thunder as he looked down at her and the blade he'd held at her throat had been all business.

"Hmm, I got lost?" she tried, watching as he let her go and backed up, crossing his arms over his massive chest. Somehow, here in this enclosed space, he seemed even bigger and she struggled to draw breath.

"Try again, little human," he rumbled, his expression unchanged. "Wearing an oonat robe, I'd say getting lost was the last thing on your mind."

The silence stretched between them; a hard, uncompromising silence and this time she did shiver, rubbing her hands up and down her arms. She hadn't had a plan beyond getting aboard, which she now realized was the dumbest thing ever. For all she knew that storage compartment might have been vented to space during take-off.

Crap, she just wasn't cut out for this espionage lifestyle. Give her an assault rifle and a battle plan any day.

"I wanted to know what had you disappearing off. I honestly didn't expect to get this far," she admitted. "I expected to get caught before I reached the shuttle. You really do need to review your security procedures. As myself, I couldn't get anywhere near the restricted sections but put on one of these?" She plucked at the robe. "And I walked right in."

"Right."

His expression grew darker, more forbidding, as though she said something wrong. Which didn't make sense. She'd told the truth, what more did he want?

"So you admit you've been spying for your people?"

For a moment she just looked at him. Then she laughed. "Of *course*, I'm damn well spying. I'm a soldier. I'm going to gather whatever intel I can. What else did you expect?"

He moved faster than she expected, grabbing her by her upper arms with a growl. "You stupid female, do you know the punishment for spying in the empire?"

She opened her mouth to answer, shaking her head, but he didn't let her get a word out.

"Flogging, with an energy whip. Fifteen lashes." Each word was punctuated with a little shake, his fingers digging hard enough into her arms to make her wince. "Most warriors don't make ten. A human? A female? *Draanth,* it would kill you."

He pushed her away to pace the cabin, shoving a shaking hand through his long hair. "Gods, I didn't want to believe them when they told me you were passing messages to that soft-bellied male. I didn't think you were so..." He looked her up and down and the expression in his eyes made her cheeks burn. "Dishonorable. I thought you were a real warrior."

She gathered her stolen robes, mangling them with her hands as she looked at him. All of a sudden, it mattered what he thought of her. Something inside her died when he looked at her that way like she was something that had crawled out from under a rock. Her throat tightened, but she ignored it and lifted her head.

"Are you going to turn me in?"

He paused his pacing to glare at her. A muscle in the corner of his jaw jumped as he looked at her. Finally, he sighed and shook his head.

"No. I don't have the time. *But,*" he barked, cutting off her sigh of relief, "you're not out of the woods yet, little human. When we get back, they're going to question you. And you're going to tell them that you stowed away because you couldn't bear to be parted from me."

Jane froze, and lifted her gaze to his hard, multicolored one. "You're going to use this to force your claim on me?"

Her words were hard, but inside she trembled. Wasn't this what she wanted, the decisions removed from her? Faced with the possibility they might be, she suddenly realized that yes, having the decision meant a great deal to her indeed.

His jaw worked, lips compressing. "No. I do not need to force any female, much less a short, stubborn, pain in the ass human female with no concept of honor. You merely need to tell them you pursued me to get me to claim you, but I declined."

"Oh great, so I'm a bunny-boiler now, am I?"

"I do not understand this phrase 'bunny-broiler.'"

He'd moved closer, one eyebrow raised and she was suddenly reminded that however much the Lathar looked like humanity, they were very different. More graceful, faster, stronger. If the two species were related, then humanity had definitely gotten the shitty end of the stick.

"Boiler," she corrected automatically. "It means an older woman who is emotionally unstable and possibly dangerous when it comes to relationships."

"You're not old." His expression was hard to read, but she thought she caught a glimmer of amusement. "I can't say anything about unstable, and we both know you're dangerous."

She just looked at him. It couldn't have escaped the Lathar's notice that she was at least fifteen years older than the other women they'd captured. In fact, a few eyebrows had raised when she requested assignment to Sentinel Five, along with a few muttered comments about her being "past it."

"I'm forty-three years old," she said flatly. "Welcome to bunny-boiler territory, and according to some of the base staff talk, practically in my dotage."

After having given her age in such a matter-of-fact manner, the last thing she expected was for him to burst into laughter.

"Really? Forty-three? Hells, you're practically a baby." He grinned, shoving his hair back with a large hand. She caught her breath, arousal surging through her as he looked up, the smile transforming his cruelly-handsome face to something more boyish. "I'm sixty-seven next month."

～

"SERIOUSLY, SIXTY-SEVEN?" Hours later, Jane still couldn't believe how old Karryl was. "I wouldn't have said more than what... thirty-five, at the most."

The big Latharian warrior sat in the opposite recliner at the front of the cockpit, his gaze focused on the holographic screens in front of him. She had to admit, seeing him stretched out like that, with his attention elsewhere was more than handy. She could look her fill without him noticing.

"Yes, sixty-seven. Do human women ever stop talking?" he grumbled, throwing a scowl her way, which she ignored.

"Be thankful I'm not Kenna. That woman can talk the hind legs off a donkey. Creatures like your *kervasi,* but smaller, and more beasts of burden rather than to ride elegantly."

He did look at her that time, his expression quizzical. "Their legs detach? That seems a strange evolutionary feature. Is that common on your planet?"

"No, they don't really come off. It's just an expression," she chuckled, rocking back on the comfortable recliner and hugging her knees. The co-pilot's couch was just as big as the pilot's and built for the Lathar, so it was almost the size of a bed. "It means she talks a lot. Nothing to do with animals at all. I actually don't know where that phrase comes from. One of my old combat sergeants used to say it."

His hands moved over the display in front of him. They'd dropped out of FTL a while back and were approaching L-three with Karryl piloting, but she knew his attention was on her.

"You've been a warrior a long time?"

"Since I was eighteen."

She glanced out the view screen. This area of space was beautiful. Big gas giants with more rings than she'd ever seen cosied up to huge white-violet nebulae. Most of that was secondary, though, to the vast asteroid field they currently picked their delicate way through. Well, rather, *he* was now picking a way through. She had no idea how to pilot the alien craft and, to be honest, her one and only flying lesson in a beat-up troop carrier had ended badly. Her instructor leaped from the ship as soon as they'd touched down, swearing never to get into anything she was piloting. Ever again.

"Joined up the day I left school. A city kid, from one of the less salubrious areas. Money and food were tight. Joining meant I got three squares a day and could send money back to feed my siblings."

He glanced across at her. "Did your parents not have sons to send instead? Why send a female?"

Her hard look went unnoticed as the consoles bleeped and claimed his attention again.

"My brother at that time was four. A little young to be sent to basic training." She sighed, and rubbed her hand down her calf. "He became a soldier in the end. He'd have been twenty-nine now."

"Been?" Karryl asked as he neatly maneuvered them around a large asteroid. They were almost at the end of the rocky field and a large satellite rotated slowly in the clear space ahead of them.

"Yeah, lost him in the colony wars," she replied briefly, sliding forward to the edge of her couch as the satellite got larger. "Is that it?"

Even with her limited knowledge of Latharian technology, it looked wrong. The sleek metal looked misshapen. Not burnt and destroyed but more like it had been melted. "That doesn't look good at all."

"No. I'm pinging it, but it's totally non-responsive. Scanning now..." His lips compressed into a thin line. His hands moved over the holo display, tapping on the thin lines in mid-air. The engines kicked in, slowing the shuttle in front of the satellite. "There's nothing left—Oh, fuck!"

Swearing in Lathar too quickly for her to

understand, his hands flew over the controls. The engines roared to life, the ship lurching as they raced away from the satellite. The sudden movement dumped her into the foot well in front of the co-pilot's couch with a yelp.

She clambered onto the couch and strapped herself in, just in case Karryl felt the need to hit the gas again. "What's going on?"

"It's emitting high levels of *keraton* radiation." His face was pale as the lights in the cabin turned orange, blinking from the cockpit to the rear. "Running a de-com routine now. The shuttle is shielded but I don't want to take any chances—"

*With her. S*he finished his sentence silently, realizing that he wasn't worried about himself, but about the effect of radiation on her. His concern was touching. Actually, rather unexpected.

"Is it dangerous?" Keeping her voice light, she pretended to double-check her harness. "We weren't in range long enough for it to have an effect, surely?"

"No." The little muscle at the side of his jaw worked again as he shook his head. "We weren't, thankfully. It's not overly dangerous to a male my size, especially with the shielding on this thing, but I don't wish to risk a female."

"You're a big softy really, aren't you?" She teased

him to lighten the mood. "So boss, the thing's toast. What's the next move?"

"Well, there are only a few species that have *keraton* technology, and given the damage, they couldn't have gotten far. There's a trading outpost not far from here. We might be able to pick up some gossip on who's been in the area, then get back within range of long distance comms to report back to the palace."

The engines rose in pitch as Karryl turned the shuttle and laid in a new course. There was a slight lurch as the FTL drives kicked in and then she found herself looking at streaks of light as the stars raced past.

"So," she grinned, relieved that they weren't going back to the palace, and the probability she'd have to face the music, "we get a road trip."

ot far from here turned out to be a two-hour journey. Lulled by the soothing hum of the engines and the lure of the comfortable recliner, years of military training to rest when she could, ensured that Jane slipped into a light doze.

A change in the sound of the engines as they dropped out of FTL woke her and she sat up, blinking and ruffling her hair so it wasn't flat. Pure feminine vanity. She'd lived in trenches and barracks for months at a time and never bothered about her appearance. For some reason with Karryl it was an entirely different matter.

"Coming up on the outpost now," the big warrior announced, his voice low and gruff. He hadn't slept but didn't appear fatigued at all. A comment

Daaynal had made a few days ago came to mind. The Lathar were experts at tinkering with genetic code, much like humans would alter and enhance vehicles, they did to themselves. They'd increased their strength, endurance, and cognitive abilities to make them better warriors.

Diseases though had proven more difficult. Curing one had changed something else and caused a worse mutation, one of which had wiped out their women. Proof positive in her mind that trying to play God bit you in the ass eventually.

But they'd created humanity. She still struggled to get her head around that revelation. That she was from the same genetic stock as Karryl, albeit it a Lathar mission a millennia ago that had been genetically engineered for different conditions. Not conditions on earth, but another planet. Something had gone wrong and they'd lost contact with the mission. It had been assumed they'd all died. Not found a new planet and survived, the memory of where they had come from lost over time and new legends and stories growing up to explain that ever-present existential question.

"It's..." Jane paused for a moment as she considered the best way to describe the outpost. A hulking mass, it was comprised of what looked like old earth storage shipping containers, hexagonal in shape, clustered around a central tube-like core. Other constructions rose from the center, tethered by metal stalks that themselves had extra structures bolted to them. Nothing matched. It looked like it had been salvaged from some intergalactic junkyard and bolted together.

A bulge at the top had to contain the docking bays by the look of the large doors on the side. Karryl turned the small shuttle toward it, then flicked her a quick glance. "Be quiet. I want them to think I'm alone."

She nodded, trying to maintain a professional expression when inside she was ready to squeal like a big kid. She was going to see aliens. Real aliens on a real alien space station. Wild west in space kind of stuff. Of course, the Lathar were aliens, but they were so human-like at times...and now it had been discovered that they and humanity were related, could they actually be called aliens?

Perhaps the real little green men were on this space station. She couldn't wait to find out.

"*Pernassis,* this is shuttle *Lei'anna* requesting permission to dock." Karryl's voice had changed from the one he usually used when speaking to her, and was firm, deep and brooked no argument. Once again she was reminded he was far more dangerous than she took him for at times.

"*Lei'anna,* this is *Pernassis,*" the reply came in a female voice that dripped sex. "We have you with a Latharian palace tag, are you sure you're not lost out here, honey?"

"That is correct, and the Lathar are never lost." Karryl almost barked the reply, obviously in no mood to play games. "I have business on the outpost. Are you going to give me permission to dock, or do I have to come back with a war group?"

There was a small squeak in reply. "No, no, there won't be any need for that. Permission to dock granted, *Lei'anna,* you're allocated to bay seven. Have a pleasant stay on *Pernassis.*"

"I sincerely hope so," Karryl left the subtle threat hanging in the air for a moment, then said. "*Lei'anna* out."

As he closed the connection, Jane lifted her eyebrow. "You Lathar are bullies, you know that? There was no need to bully that poor woman like that."

"Bully? A Krin?" He chuckled, shaking his head. "Not likely. That *poor woman* is the male of 'her' species, taller than most Lathar, with eight arms and a fondness for the flesh of other species, preferably served raw and screaming."

"Shiiiit." Jane shivered. "She sounded like a phone sex worker."

Karryl nodded, movements sure on the controls as he took them into the docking bay. Obviously he got the reference. "That's how they hunt. Pheromones and sex appeal. Their scent glands fetch a high price for use in the perfumery industry. The trouble is they tend to be rather attached to their body parts, so harvesting them to sell is a high-risk occupation. A well-paying one if you can avoid getting slaughtered and eaten. I do believe some of them prey on their own for that reason."

She blinked in surprise. "What? They kill their own to sell their scent glands?"

He shrugged, turning the shuttle about neatly and easing them into bay seven. At least, she assumed it was bay seven. The painted number on the metal bulkhead in front of them had long since worn off. There was a small bump as they hit the docking clamps, then a whir and clunk as the clamps engaged. A wave of Karryl's hand killed the shuttle's engines.

"It's economical when you think about it. Get paid for the glands, the rest they eat."

She covered her mouth for a moment. "That's just sick."

Karryl unbuckled his harness and levered himself out of the recliner. The holo-consoles snapped off at his movement. "Not every species has humanity's morals. Spend any time out here and you'll learn that. Fast, if you want to survive."

"So I'm finding out."

She unbuckled, and tumbled off the couch, following him to the back of the cabin. Lathar were always armed, but he opened a door on the side of the cabin, the handle recessed like the rest, to reveal a weapons cache. Whistling through her teeth, she looked along the racked weaponry. For a two man shuttle, it sure was well stocked.

Already carrying a heavy pistol holstered on his hip and blades nestled in his boots and wrist sheaths, Karryl picked out a second gun belt. He buckled it about his hips and added not one but two pistols. Huh, double-decker holster, that was neat. She looked for another one but could only see a standard belt with a holster on each hip.

Karryl paused, what looked like a shotgun in his hand, as she picked up the belt. "What do you think you're doing?"

Giving him a "well, duh" look, she buckled the

belt. There weren't enough holes so it didn't fit snugly, sliding down to wedge over her hips at a slant. "Arming up. There's no way I'm walking onto an alien space station without a shit-load of weaponry."

He plucked the pistol she'd picked up out of her hands and shoved it back into its slot. His look could have melted perma-steel. "Oh, no, you're not. I am not riski—"

Fury surged. She snatched the gun out and jumped down his throat before he could get another word out. "Because I'm a woman? I'm a goddamn soldier, this is what I do!"

He hissed in anger and frustration, showing his teeth.

"I meant risking the *mission*. These people have never seen a human. You'll stand out like a fucking sore thumb." He plucked the weapon from her fingers and jammed it back, shaking the rack. "Not everything's about you. I need to get information, not announce our fucking presence to all aboard."

Fuck. She hadn't thought about it like that. Silent, she took a step back and nodded. There was no way she wanted to interfere with his mission. She was already on a sticky wicket where the palace was concerned because of her attempts to spy for Terran

Command, she didn't need to compound her errors. Her desire to see little green men would just have to wait.

"I apologize, you're perfectly correct. I'll stay here and guard the ship."

He nodded, swinging what looked like the lathar version of a shotgun over his shoulder. Or a grenade launcher, it looked like it could be either or both.

"Ship, activate surveillance perimeter on my bio-signature."

"Affirmative," a disembodied voice made Jane jump and look around.

The holo-consoles in the cockpit reactivated, casting a blue glow over the two control couches. There were two images: one showing a corridor with an airlock door, and the other showing the two of them standing in the middle of the shuttle's cabin. At the same moment, the door opened onto the airlock.

"The ship's AI will track me as I move through the station," he explained, taking a step forward to tuck a finger under her chin and lift it so she had to meet his eyes. Her breath caught as he loomed over her. Not through fear. Something else surged through her veins. She preferred him like this, as he really was, rather than trying to be civilized to charm her into his bed.

The ghost of a smile whispered over his lips. "You'll get to see your little green men."

She hadn't told him that. Her eyes narrowed, but he smiled. "You talk in your sleep, little one."

Before she could argue, he bent and kissed her. It was firm, but brief, the contact ended before she'd registered it.

"Stay here, don't touch anything and behave. I don't want to have to explain to Daaynal if something happens to his ship."

With that, he left the shuttle, door closing behind him.

Jane stayed where she was for a moment, lifting her hand to her lips. They tingled from his kiss, every time he touched her. Frustration surged through her. She liked him, a lot, and she knew he wanted her.

If he was human, she'd have jumped him in a hot minute and enjoyed every inch of that lean, hard warrior's body. Then, when whatever they had worked itself out, they could have parted amicably, as friends. But he was lathar so it wasn't that simple. If she shared his bed, accepted his claim, that was it...they were joined for a lifetime. And that scared the living crap out of her.

But he wasn't pushing his claim anymore, which confused her. The man was a born predator so she knew he hadn't given up, doubted he even knew the meaning of the concept. No, he was playing another game, one she hadn't figured out yet, and her blood thrilled at the thought.

Sighing, she ran a hand through her hair and headed for the cockpit with its twin displays. No time to figure out what he was up to now; she'd have to bide her time.

The pilot's couch was just as comfortable as the co-pilot's, but her attention was less on the padding beneath her posterior, and all on the big man displayed on the screens in front of her. For a moment, he dominated both as he stepped out of the airlock and walked down the corridor away from the ship. The image on the right shifted to another camera and she could see Karryl walking toward her, his expression grim and forbidding, while the picture on the left showed the empty corridor outside the airlock door.

The images changed as he moved through the ship, the AI moving from one camera to another to keep him in view. As he entered the main area of the outpost, which looked like a mall back home, Jane got her first view of aliens in the "wild." There were two levels to the main promenade, the upper with wraparound balconies that looked down on the lower. A line of dried out fountains in the center of the ground level gave hints toward more auspicious times, long since passed.

Both levels were packed with creatures of all shapes and sizes. Tall, yeti-like creatures walked next to what looked like a blob of pink slime. She recognized one of the more insectoid creatures as the same species from the Latharian palace, and there were many oonat, mostly on leashes. The poor creatures appeared to be everyone's whipping boy.

One thing she didn't miss was that Karryl was the only Lathar aboard, and everyone was quick to scuttle out of his way. She didn't blame them. There was an aura of lethality around the big warrior that no one in their right mind wanted to mess with.

"Stop," she said suddenly, catching something in the corner of the screen. "Can you roll that back a little, or expand the view?"

"Affirmative," the AI replied smoothly and the screen on the right grew in size, moving the airlock corridor one up above, as the camera panned out.

"There and there," Jane pointed to two dark-clothed figures in the crowds behind Karryl. "I've seen them too much. Are they following him?"

"Assessing..."

The AI split the screen again so there were now three views. The corridor above, Karryl moving through the crowds on the left while on the right, the AI flicked rapidly through different images from the outpost camera feeds. Each image concentrated on one of the men she'd pointed out.

"There is a 97.375 percent probability the subjects are following Warrior Karryl," the AI said, its voice unemotional. "Analysis of physical movements suggests subjects are likely to be *Krynassis* mercenaries."

"What the hell are they?"

Jane's heart rate picked up as the two closed in on the unaware Karryl. He'd entered a bar on the second level and appeared to be in conversation with an insectoid. His back was to the entrance of the bar, which made all her soldier instincts scream. He was an open target.

"Regardless of their physical location, the Krynassis are a highly dangerous reptilian-derived lifeform with similar physical capabilities to the Lathar."

Helpfully, the AI changed the image on the right

side of the screen and a new face appeared. It was male, with close-cropped short hair and at first glance could have been mistaken for human or lathar. Then she noticed the shimmer of scales over the high cheekbones, and as the man in the image smiled, the sharp fangs. Still, he wouldn't have looked out of place as a male centerfold. For ladies into scales...

"Shit, why are all aliens freaking hot?"

"The Krynassis are cold-blooded," the AI interjected. "Pack hunters, they are considered extremely dangerous in hand-to-hand combat."

Karryl was on his own and unaware he was being stalked.

"What are Karryl's chances on his own?" she asked bluntly. Sliding off the seat, she strode across the cabin and yanked the weapons cache open. Her hands were steady as she armed up. There was no way she was allowing those lizard men to take him down. Not without going through her first.

The ship's voice continued. "Poor. Alone, he is likely to sustain life-threating injuries. However," she heard the disapproval in the computer's voice, "his chances will not be improved by the addition of an inferior being to protect."

Jane paused, pistol in hand and looked at the

consoles. She isolated the AI's location at the front of the craft, given away by a small blinking blue light whenever it "spoke."

"You want to run that by me again?" she asked, eyebrow raised. "Inferior being? And before you answer, I would invite you to consider that this *inferior being* has an energy weapon and a direct line of sight to your processor housing."

The AI was silent for a few seconds, then the lights flickered again. "Point taken. May I suggest some...enhancements?"

There was a click and a door to the left of the weapons cache slid to the side. A rack smoothly extended from the dark space within and Jane sucked in a breath. Body armor, but not like she'd ever see. This stuff was bad-ass and made of the same metal as the combat bots the K'Vass used to attack Sentinel Five. Pity the shuttle was too small to carry any of them.

"Armor?" she asked, already unbuckling her gun belts to put on the stuff.

The lower half hit the floor with a clunk and she turned so that she could step back into it. The small of her back hit the belt and the whole thing moved, adjusting to her more diminutive stature as harnesses snapped around her legs and tightened.

She lifted a leg experimentally. Despite the metal and straps, she didn't feel any different.

"Combat exoskeleton," the AI replied. "Designed to enhance a warrior's performance on the battlefield. It should overcome your natural...limitations."

Its speech pattern had changed, becoming more fluid and...human. It was mimicking her, Jane realized.

"You learn fast. I'll give you that."

Jane grinned as she lifted the breastplate over her head and settled it on her shoulders. Like the lower half, as soon as it sensed it was in the right place it started to adjust. Straps shot from the sides and wrapped around her torso, hooking into loops on the leg portion and pulled tight. A flap on the shoulders flipped down and with a *click-click-click* a row of plates not unlike scales covered her arms.

"So I should," the AI sounded huffy, as though she'd insulted its intelligence. "My brain patterns were modeled after one of the greatest mathematical engineers in Latharian history, Miisan K'Vass."

"Tarrick's mother?" She'd heard Cat mention the name.

The AI made a small noise. "And sister to the emperor. She was beloved by all and a genius. A lot of the technology currently used by the Lathar was developed from her work. Mathematics was a great passion amongst women of her class before the plague took them from us."

Great. She'd always had the impression Latharian women were delicate, frail creatures who needed looking after, not freaking geniuses. Mathematics was not her strong point, unless they were talking enemy numbers and how much ammunition she had left. Anything past the mundane and she was lost. The fact that the women Karryl had grown up with were highly intelligent made her feel even more like the dumb grunt she was.

"A helmet too?" She cleared her throat, covering her discomfort and reached for it.

"Indeed. It should conceal your gender although there is nothing we can do about your physical size. Since no one will expect you to be female, most will assume you are a younger warrior."

"Good."

At least her hair would be covered. In the palace, nearly everyone seemed fascinated by the short, platinum locks. Blond was an uncommon color amongst the Lathar. The only one she'd seen so far was the emperor's champion, Xaandril.

Helmet in place, she blinked as the screen showing Karryl in the bar appeared at the bottom right of her field of vision. It alternated with the view outside the bar where the mercenaries were gathering. She needed to move. Now.

"Seal the airlock behind me," she ordered, grabbing her weaponry. The exosuit moved, providing holsters so she loaded up. Never could have too many guns. Not when going into a hot situation that involved lizard men. Perhaps she should take a mouse or two as a distraction. "Don't open the doors for anyone but me and Karryl."

"Understood. And Jane?"

She stopped halfway out of the door and looked back. The cockpit screens had changed to show the face of a Latharian woman. Tall, she was ethereally beautiful and Jane knew she was looking at a facsimile of Miisan K'Vass.

"Yes?"

The AI woman smiled. "Good luck."

6

*K*arryl had been in many low down, disgusting dives in his adult life, but *Pernassis* beat them all, hands down. He shouldn't have expected anything else though. This area of space was a no man's land between sectors, well off the main space lanes. An area of lawlessness and chaos most people avoided.

A small smile curved his lips at the thought of the stubborn, beautiful little human woman. Well, little next to him anyway...she was the tallest amongst the earth women he'd seen so far.

"So, have you seen my cousin, or not?" he demanded, glaring down at the *Kalaxian* bartender on the other side of the counter.

Small, overweight, and universally bald, there

was no way of knowing whether the creature was male or female. Even other Kalaxians had trouble working that out.

Whatever gender it was, there were two constants about Kalaxians. Thanks to a near religious knowledge of alcoholic drinks they were usually employed as bartenders, and they loved to gossip. A perfect combination. If anyone wanted to know anything, all they had to do was head to the nearest bar and hit up a purple-skin for information.

"Your cousin, you say?"

This particular purple-skin was shrewd, beady little eyes far too perceptive as they wandered over him, lingering over his chest and trailing down his abdomen to his groin. *Draanth,* he hoped this one wasn't female. They weren't particular about the species of their sexual partners if they were in heat or much concerned with consent. Just breathing the same air could be considered a yes.

"Cousin. Twice removed." He kept his voice firm, altering his posture to loom a little. "Took off in a flyer a week ago. It was an expensive bit of kit, we'd like it back. Him as well, if he hasn't managed to kill himself."

"Well..." The bartender edged forward, a primary hand swiping a dirty cloth over the counter at the same time one of the secondary arms just beneath shoved a proto-paw out in an unspoken demand. "There may been some warriors through here recently. But they looked more J'nuut than K'Vass. You *are* K'Vass, aren't you?"

Karryl narrowed his eyes. Like any warrior on a hush-hush mission, he'd been careful to remove all identifying markers from his leathers before he'd left. The braids in his hair marked him as a senior warrior, but the fact that the Kalaxian identified his family affiliation so easily rang alarm bells. Unlike most of his clan, Karryl didn't bear the traditional K'Vass features.

"I could be, depends on who wants to know." He changed tactics, relaxing his body language to lean on the bar and press a credit chip into the creature's paw. His lips curved into a small smile designed to charm and beguile. "Why do you ask?"

The creature's purple skin flushed yellow, not a pleasant combination, and the fluttering of its eyelashes confirmed his suspicions that it was female. Great, he could charm the pants off a four armed purple-skinned blob, but not the woman who sat safely in his shuttle.

His life sucked.

The Kalaxian pulled a glass from under the bar,

filled it with something from one of the taps that looked more like black sludge than anything remotely palatable.

"Certain friends have asked to be informed of your arrival," she said, her voice low as she tapped the front of the glass with a horn-like fingernail.

He flicked a glance down. The black sludge had turned the simple glass into a highly reflective surface. One good enough for him to spot the three dark figures sneaking up from behind.

Draanth. Hand closing around the glass, he turned and threw it at the nearest of his opponents. A glimpse of scales and a hiss as the man ducked, the black sludge cascading over his hooded head and shoulders told Karryl they were Krynassis mercs. Crap, lizard men were pricey and there were three on his tail, which meant someone out there really didn't want anyone asking questions.

The other two rushed him at the same time, their mouths wide to reveal vicious fangs. Dropping to the ground, he swept a hard leg out to drop one and shoved the bar stool into the path of the other. The first went down hard, rolling away just as Karryl stamped hard where his face had been a moment before.

He didn't waste time, spinning around and

bringing his guard up just in time to stop a scaly fist slamming into the side of his head. Twisting his wrist, he grabbed the lizard man's hand, trapping him with his arm extended. A practiced flick dropped a blade into his hand and he sliced at the guy's rib cage.

The krynassis grunted. Wet heat cascading over Karryl's hand told him his blade had struck true. Snarling, he planted a booted foot in the center of the creature's chest and kicked him away. The merc went down, sliding in his own blood to curl up under the nearest table.

One down, two to... The door banged again and three more lizards stalked through, their yellow gaze fixed on him.

Just fucking great. More lizard men to the party. And they ran in packs, so if there were a few, there were definitely more around. He pulled his blaster and pulled the trigger. Nothing. Just a flat *ppphsttt.* Shit, they had a mobile suppression field.

"Oh, so this is how it is?" He backed up, making sure they couldn't get behind him. With a pack, he couldn't hope to hold them off indefinitely. Which meant this was going to hurt. A lot. "Okay, who wants to dance first? I warn you, I don't intend to make this easy."

"Good." The nearest added a hiss to the end of the word. "We prefer the prey fights back. And it's been a long time since any of us tasted Lathar blood."

Karryl curled his lips back, showing his teeth. "Come and get it then, if you think you're tough enough."

Hisses filled the bar, the rest of the patrons having wisely cleared out, and the five mercenaries rushed him at once. Within seconds, he was fighting for his life. His existence narrowed down to each kick and slash, to the physical exertion required to block each punch thrown his way.

His senses expanded, hyper-alert to every movement from the men around him. He didn't bother with any of the flourishes or showing off that he might have done against a lesser enemy, or back in the court to impress the woman he yearned to claim as his own.

Jane, the thought filled his head as he fought and he bellowed in rage. If he fell here, she would be alone, on an alien outpost. That was not happening.

One jumped on his back, fangs perilously close to his neck and he fell backward, landing heavily on it. There was a crunch and a scream, but the move left him on his back, his belly exposed to the others.

A hard, scaly arm wrapped around his neck. He struggled like a wild *deearin*, trying to get loose, but they fell on him as a pack. There were more than five now, way more than five.

Fists slammed into his unprotected abdomen, no claws yet, but that would come. It was just a matter of time.

Then one was ripped away from him. Its grunt of surprise changed to a scream of pain as bone crunched and the smell of lizard blood blossomed into the air. He took advantage of the lizards' momentary distraction to heave them all off and flip to his feet. Slamming his fist into the side of a scaled skull, he cast a glance to the side to check who his unexpected savior could be. He hadn't seen anyone on his way here who looked like they would be an ally. A few might consider the Lathar owing them a favor worth the risk of tangling with a pack of Krynassis though.

It wasn't a mercenary. Instead, another Latharian warrior, fully armored, fought beside him with a level of skill that took Karryl's breath away. Lithe and fast, he was too small to be an adult. He could only be a youth, not yet attained his full growth. As he watched, the boy took on two of the krynassis at once, combining punches and kicks in a manner he'd never seen before but lethally effective. One lizard ran at him from behind and Karryl opened his mouth to shout a warning. It wasn't needed.

The youth flicked a glance over his shoulder, and with a hard right hook to the jaw of the one in front of him, he dropped to his knees to slam a foot backward. There was a crunch as the mercenary's knee went the wrong way. He fell and the young warrior followed him, grabbing an arm as he went. With a roll and tuck, he wrapped his legs around the lizard man's torso, holding his arms out of the way. Gloved hands gripped the creature's skull and without a moment's pause, he wrenched it sharply, snapping the neck. Shoving the body away, he rolled back to his feet again, facing off against another opponent.

Young he might be, but he was a true warrior.

The fight took Karryl's attention again, and he put his back to the younger warrior, confident they could take on any number of krynassis that turned up. With a bellow, he dodged and weaved, looking for gaps in their defence and hitting hard. Ribs, noses, joints...they all cracked beneath his fists. Grunts of pain and the occasional scream filled the air, all from the lizard men. Eventually, the few who were left backed off, then ran for the door, scrambling over each other to get away from the two lathar.

They both stood for a moment, breathing heavily. Leaning forward, Karryl rested his hands on his thighs to ease his bruised abdomen. Looking up, he nodded to his new companion.

"Well met, friend. My thanks for your assistance. Without it, the outcome here would not have been as good."

Carefully, he avoided mention of his ship and the fact he had a female companion. Most Lathar knew of the existence of the human race now, and that they had women. As young a male as this one appeared to be, Karryl didn't fancy ending up in a challenge fight with him. Even though he wore body armor, honor dictated the enhancement levels were set to minimal, so he'd be just as lethal out of it.

Straightening, he offered his arm, palm up, for a warrior's handclasp.

The youth didn't move. His faceplate completely concealed his expression but for a moment Karryl could have sworn he was surprised. Perhaps not a stretch of the imagination. If he was not yet a warrior and this was his proving mission, he wouldn't have expected to be treated as a full-fledged warrior.

"For your assistance, I'll happily vouch for your first warrior's braid." Karryl smiled, hand still out.

His smile remained in place as the kid bent his head and lifted his hands to remove the helmet. He waited for a look at the youth's face. Most Lathar clans bore a distinct family resemblance and fought in similar styles, but he couldn't identify the style this one had used. So which clan had he come from? Certainly not one of the bigger ones. Perhaps a back-system clan? Instantly, he dismissed the thought. The armor looked to be top of the range, a type Karryl had never seen before. But then, the K'Vass preferred not to use armor at all...

His hair was blond, nearly white and cropped short. Karryl frowned. There weren't many light-haired Lathar and a warrior in training should have long hair, not shor—

The breath hissed out of his lungs as his companion lifted her head.

"Jane."

Surprise held him captive for a moment, as he tried to make his brain absorb everything. The lethal young warrior he'd mentally been congratulating a moment ago was a female. *His* female.

His female had just taken on a horde of Krynassis mercenaries and kicked their asses.

"What the fuck did you think you were doing, woman? You could have been killed!" Her mouth dropped open in shock as he grabbed her helmet and jammed it back on her head. "Put that back on, before someone sees you."

Fury and fear rolled through him in equal amounts. She shouldn't be here. Not out in the open like this. If other races knew there was a human out here, female or not, there would be a bloodbath. They'd band together, kill him, and sell her on the auction block to the highest bidder. Fuck, there was a Krin on board... that fucker would bankrupt its entire pod for a new species to "sample."

His body shook with suppressed rage and the fear of what could have happened. Hand hard on her arm, he frog marched her from the bar and through the crowded promenade.

"What the fuck, Karryl!" she hissed, trying to get free but he didn't let go. If anything, his grip tightened.

The crowds scattered before them, but he didn't care. All that mattered was getting her back to the ship. To make sure she was safe. The need to protect her, even though she'd shown herself more than capable, was like the need to breathe. He didn't have a choice.

"Let me go, you idiot!" She didn't give up, struggling all the way back to the docking ring and the corridor outside their airlock. "I saved your life!"

"By putting yourself in danger," he snarled, shoving her through the airlock door as soon as it opened. They'd barely cleared the first door than the second was already opening, so he pushed her through that as well.

She stumbled into the main cabin, tearing the helmet from her head as soon as the door was shut to glare at him. If looks could kill, he'd be colder than stone.

"What the hell are you playing at? Is this the thanks I get for saving your life?"

"At the risk to your own!" Now they were alone, he didn't bother to regulate his tone.

His bellow made her wince but not back down. Anger flared in her eyes.

"Risk? What risk? I can take care of myself!"

"Really?"

He stilled, all the heat of his anger draining into something else. Something far more dangerous. For her. Taking a step forward, he crowded her against the wall. Deliberately invaded her space to threaten her. His lip curled back a little.

"Prove it, little female."

Without giving her further warning, he attacked. Her gasp of surprise was audible, but she got a block up in time, stopping his blow to her ribs just in time. She was armored, so he didn't bother pulling his punches. The exo-suit would take the brunt of the blows.

The fight was fast and furious, ranging through the tiny cabin and around the extended bed. She was quick, blocking his blows with a speed and strength that surprised him. Some of it was the suit, but not all. He'd always known she was a good soldier, lethal with a rifle, but she was also formidable in hand-to-hand combat.

Even with the suit to help her, he was bigger, faster, stronger, and better. He pressed his advantage ruthlessly, blocking each try she made to get away from him and out of the corner he'd penned her into. The only advantage he let her have was that he couldn't bring himself to hit her in the face. Just the arcas he knew would be shielded by the armor,

She fought silently, her expression a blank mask even though he knew some of his blows had to hurt. That she shielded her pain made him proud; that he'd been the one to cause it made him ashamed.

He'd never lifted a hand to a female in his life...

He spotted the opening before it happened,

reading the movement of her body to gauge the exact moment she dropped her guard a little on the left and struck. The solid blow to her solar plexus made her reel back, her face suddenly pale and tight with pain. Not giving her chance to recover, he moved in, wrapping up her arms and falling backward with her onto the extended bed.

Within a heartbeat, he'd twisted and had her pinned beneath him. Hissing, she tried to buck him off, but her struggles were weaker than a day old *deearin*. She tried to punch him so he captured her hands, pinning one above her head and the other against her body.

"Ready to give in?" he asked softly, riding out her bucking and thrashing until she quietened. Her gaze latched onto his, both colors cold and jewel-like.

"Lesson delivered and assimilated." Her voice was clipped, angry. "Thank you for the life re-adjustment."

Her anger didn't put him off. Rather it clashed with his own and fed it, then fed an entirely different type of rage. He shouldn't, he knew he shouldn't, but the urge to taste her again consumed him. Dipping his head, his mouth crashed down on hers in a hard kiss fueled by the fear and rage that coursed through his blood.

He expected her to stiffen. Expected her to freeze him out and lie stiff beneath him, but she didn't. Instead, she kissed him back, meeting his anger with a fury of her own. Matched him, challenged him, and when he paused, nipped his lower lip.

Lust shot through him. His gasp was lost beneath their kiss as he moved. Sliding one leg between both of hers, he tore at the breastplate of the armor, desperate to get it off her and feel her soft curves beneath. How he could have thought her a male he had no idea. His cock certainly knew the difference. It was as stiff as a support strut and throbbed against the constraint of his leathers.

The straps retracted and she raised her shoulders, toned stomach crunched to allow him to lift the armor clear. He discarded it on the floor, the lower section following a moment later. Passion shrouded his vision and his common sense. It didn't matter to him that she wouldn't accept his claim, he had to touch her, had to taste her and prove to himself that she was safe. Protected in his arms. *His.*

Her hands moved over his chest. Reaching up, he yanked the zipper free, desperate to feel her caress. The knowledge that she found him attractive... that she wanted to touch him made him swell all the more.

Despite all his instincts roaring at him to push her back and take her, make her accept his claim, he held still to let her explore. His brain blanked, short-circuited by the movement of her lips beneath his, the passion as she stroked her tongue against his. He'd expected her to fight, and to put him off as she had so many times before.

She wasn't saying no anymore.

He gasped as she slid her hand under his leathers to cup him boldly.

Shit, she *really* wasn't saying no anymore.

"You like that, huh?" she broke away to whisper against his lips and he nodded. The hunter had become the prey. He wasn't sure how she'd turned the tables on him so easily, but he wasn't going to argue. His entire existence narrowed to the two of them on the bed, and her hand on his cock. She stroked him with feather light touches, then firmer ones, both designed to drive him crazy.

"Yeah," he admitted throatily. "I like that."

He held the dominant position, braced on his hands as she lay in the cage of his arms, but she was in charge. No doubt about that at all. And he was a willing participant in his own submission. Her lips whispered over his. Kissing him lightly, almost innocently, her hand carrying out more carnal deeds. Blood surged, heat cascading through his veins until his body shook with the effort to keep still. Then he'd had enough. Sliding one arm under her neck and the other around her waist, he rolled until she was on top of him.

Cupping her delicate face in his hands, he threw caution to the wind and deepened the kiss, sweeping into the softer recess of her mouth with a hard tongue. She moaned in pleasure and gripped him tighter, both a boon to the ego damaged by her constant rejections.

"Undress me," he ordered, his voice thick with passion. "I want to feel your hands on me. All of me."

She nodded, eyes wide and dark and let go of his cock. He bit back a moan of disappointment, lying back to watch her as she undid his leathers. Her movements were quick and efficient. Shook with the need he saw reflected in her eyes.

Triumph wrapped around the desire surging through him. His little human wasn't as uninterested in him as she'd made out. She wanted this as much as he did. Now that he knew, he'd never let her get away with such a charade again.

The fastenings on his leathers gave and his cock sprang free to arch in a proud curve toward his stomach. So close to her, he caught the small intake of breath and the way her eyes widened suddenly. Shit, he'd known Lathar men were bigger than human, but he hadn't thought it was that much of a difference. Obviously, it was.

"Hey, shhh..." he caught her to him, reaching up to kiss her again. Long, drugging kisses to bind her to him and calm her. "I'll be gentle. Slow. I promise."

How he was going to keep that promise when her smallest touch set his entire body on fire, he didn't know, but somehow he would manage.

She nodded, her trust in him humbling. Sweeping his thumb over her delicate cheekbone, he pulled her closer. Held her as he began to undress her. So close...

"I appreciate that you're busy," the AI spoke abruptly. "But I thought you'd like to know there are twenty Krynassis in the corridor. With a cutter."

7

*J*ane froze, her gaze locked with Karryl's for a split second as the reality of their situation sank in. She saw the instant he collected himself, his gaze sharpening as he pushed her off him and leaped off the bed.

"*Draanth*, twenty?" he demanded, tucking himself in as he strode across the cabin. Jane followed, all desire quashed at the thought of those creatures getting in here. The thought of what they'd been about to do...she pushed that to the back of her mind to deal with later. *Much* later.

The AI already had a view of the corridor outside the ship on the holo display and as Jane watched, more lizard men piled in behind the three carrying what she assumed was the cutter.

"At a low estimate, yes," the AI replied dryly. "There's probably more. Records indicate there are seven Krynassis ships docked at present."

"Great, just fucking great." He dropped into the pilot's couch, hands moving in mid-air to access the pilot's controls. "Bring the engines online."

"Online and powering up."

"How many per ship? On average?" Jane asked as she slid into the co-pilot's couch and buckled herself in. The shuttle began to vibrate as the engines came up to power.

"Three clutches per ship, twenty in a clutch give or take." The AI's voice betrayed a hint of worry. "We have another issue. The docking bay doors are closing. I'm trying to countermand, but they've input an override code. Without being physically in the control room, I can't block it."

"Got it," Karryl hooked his arms under the harness on his couch and looked across at Jane. He nodded in approval when he saw she was already clipped in. "Hold on, this is going to be a bumpy ride."

She nodded, not bothering to answer and distract him. The ship surged forward, banking sharply at the same time before Karryl opened the engines to full. They hurtled toward the bay doors closing and blocking their view of the stars beyond.

"We're not going to make it," she yelled over the sound of the engines, loud in the confines of the bay. "Does this thing have weapons?"

Before she'd finished her sentence, a holo console flickered to life in front of her. She stared at it, worried that the alien technology would be beyond her. However, a target was a target, and a trigger was a trigger whatever culture a person came from, and thankfully, Latharian technology was intuitive.

With a grin, she put her hands on the screen. It was a tactile display, the light bending under her hands and forming constructs she could feel and manipulate. Focusing her gaze up, she brought both crosshairs on the screen to bear on the bay doors. They went yellow, then red, which she sure as hell hoped indicated the guns were locked on. She squeezed the triggers.

Rat-rat-rat-rat-rat-rat-rat-rat-rat-rat.

Laser bolts spat from the front of the shuttle, chewing into the metal of the bay doors as though they were soft as cheese. With a yell, she carved out a hole in the doors big enough for the shuttle to pass, removing the last hunk of metal barring their escape as they moved through.

"Nice shooting," Karryl commented, his voice tight and his focus on the screens in front of him as they roared from the outpost.

"Krynassis in pursuit," the AI informed them. "And two more incoming, bearing three-seven-alpha-five."

"Reinforcements," he commented grimly, canting the shuttle to the side as space in front of them shimmered like the haze over asphalt on a hot summer's day. One moment there was nothing there and the next two ships blinked into existence. Big, with overlapping armor plates, they looked reptilian to match their owners.

So that was what ships looked like when they came out of faster-than-light. Jane filed the information away as she aimed again.

"Take out their shield generators," Karryl ordered, swinging the ship around. "How long before we can hit FTL?"

The view through the port in front of her changed to clear space, but her screens continued to show the Krynassis ships. It was easy to identify the guns, they were the bits spitting laser fire at them, but the generators were a little more difficult.

Suddenly she spotted smaller structures set way back from the gun turrets and focused on them.

Rat-rat-rat-rat-rat-rat.

Her volley took one out, the explosion causing a shimmer over the section of the hull nearest to it. Jane grinned. Bingo.

"Thirty seconds before FTL drive fully operational."

"We can't last that long." Karryl's voice was the sort of controlled shout she knew all too well. The sound of a commanding officer who was rapidly running out of choices.

"Jump as soon as possible to the nearest suitable coordinates."

The AI was silent for a second, then said, "Affirmative. Ready to jump in five."

"Keep them off us," he ordered, pushing the engines until they screamed.

"Trying to." Her lips compressed into a thin line as she kept aiming and firing, trying to open a section on the nearest ship's shields over the engines. If she could hit an engine, then perhaps she could take both of the bigger ones out.

Space around them was live with laser bolts, each one that hit them rattling the smaller ship until she was sure the next hit would be their last.

"Jumping in four…"

Rat-rat-rat-rat-rat-rat.

"Three…"

Two more sections out. She grinned nastily and aimed for what looked like exhaust vents.

"Two…"

The crosshairs converged, laying over each other and she pulled the triggers, emptying both barrels into her target. Laser bolts slammed into it, peeling away the metal. Blue flame blossomed into space, quickly enveloping the Krynassis ship before it exploded in a beautiful and deadly display.

"One…jumping to FTL."

The shockwave from the Krynassis ships rolled toward them. Jane held her breath, praying they'd jump before it hit. She'd never seen an alien ship explode but in her experience, explosions in space where there wasn't anything to slow the shrapnel was never good.

The now familiar lurch of an FTL jump grabbed the ship. Rather than the stars around them turning to streaks of light as they sped past, they winked out of existence only to reappear almost instantaneously. The view screen was filled with a bright blue planet looming ominously in front of them. Before she could say anything, something hit them hard from behind, sending them hurtling into the upper atmosphere.

"*Draanth,* the shockwave from the explosion," Karryl yelled over the din as the ship screamed under the stresses and red alarms blared. "Boost power to the engines, we need to pull out of the atmosphere before we're too far in."

"Engines at maximum." Even the AI shouted. Jane gripped the edges of her couch as the nose of the shuttle began to glow. Shit. Shouldn't it take longer than this for them to start to burn up. "Engaging maneuvering thrusters to try and break away."

"It's no good." Karryl's face was tight, knuckles white as he tried to hold the shuttle steady. "Use them to keep us level and divert all available power to shields."

"Diverting." The lights in the cabin went out, leaving only the blue haze from the pilot's console and the red glow from outside for illumination. "Shields maxed out. At current rate, they will burn out in forty-five seconds."

"It'll have to be enough." Karryl nodded, lips compressed into a thin line. He flicked a glance to her and she read the concern in his eyes. "Hold on," he ordered. "It's going to be a rough ride."

And rough it was. The ship bucked and screamed in distress, shields white hot as they burned through the atmosphere. She squeezed her eyes shut, concentrating on controlling her breathing to ignore the panic that wanted to surge through her system. They seemed to be plummeting like a stone. Faster than she'd thought and at the same time not fast enough.

"Almost through, just a little more." Karryl's deep voice reached her, the familiar tones comforting. Despite the danger they were in, she felt safe. He wouldn't let anything happen to her. If he drew breath, he'd make sure she was safe. She knew that as sure as she knew she would take her next breath.

"Coming through now, we're saf—" His triumphant announcement was cut off as they dropped through the cloud cover only to find a cliff face looming right in front of them. The high-pitched scream as Karryl barrel-rolled the shuttle couldn't be hers, surely? She was sure it was though as they dropped like a stone.

"Brace!" Was all the warning she got as they hit the snow-covered vista below the cliff. Then they tumbled, rolling over and over. Metal screeched and her couch came free of its fixings. The view screen shattered at the same moment, dumping tons of cold snow into the cabin. Darkness and cold slammed into her, and she slipped into nothingness.

"Hhhhuhhnnnn!"

Karryl snapped back to consciousness with a sharp groan. Every part of his body hurt like he'd been on the battlefield for a week or more. For a moment, he lay where he was, doing a mental once over. Everything ached, but no one part gave the sort of deeper pain that would indicate something more serious. Cuts and bruises. And he was cold. Damn cold.

Since he'd just crashed the ship into the side of a mountain that was a pretty good outcome.

Jane.

His eyes snapped open, giving him a slanted view of the side of the cabin. His couch had come loose in the crash and flipped on its side. He was still in it though, covered with a thin layer of snow, held in place by the harness straps over his shoulders. But the space next to him, where the co-pilots couch should have been, was empty. Ragged holes in the deck showed where it had torn loose. Fear and panic forced his heart into a rapid beat. Where was she?

"*Draanth, draanth, draanth,*" he muttered, tearing at his harness and dropping to the floor.

Instantly he was on his knees, craning his neck to look around the cabin. A biting wind whipped through the shattered view screen, bringing more snow to join the rest already crammed into the small space. From the way it settled, he'd been out for a while. Humans were more susceptible to the cold than Lathar. She could have died from hypothermia while he was unconscious. A small moan forced its way past his lips.

No, she couldn't have died. He wouldn't allow it. Ever.

Scrambling across the cabin, he plunged into the snow, hands cast wide to sweep through it and discover what lay beneath. The bed was still in place, beyond it a large lump of something. The other couch upended with its broken deck brackets uppermost.

Whispering the closest thing he'd ever come to a prayer, he grabbed at it. The metal groaned, snow whipping at his face, as he managed to move it half an inch. His hands slipped, pain lancing his palm as sharp edges sliced deeply. He ignored it, pain was inconsequential when he had a mate to save.

Setting his feet more steadily, he found a better grip on the brackets and heaved again.

"Aaaarrggh!" he bellowed, putting everything he had into the movement. His arms pulled, shoulders tight as the powerful muscles in his thighs pushed to maximum. Body tensed into an arch, he held tight, waiting for that slight give from his burden.

With a crack, it moved, faster than he'd expected. With a yell of triumph, he turned it over, desperate to check on its precious cargo. It thumped to the floor, upright, with Jane fully clipped in her harness. She lay still, too still, her face turned from him. Blood covered the side he could see, crusted at her temple, and his heart skipped a beat.

"Please no..." Hands shaking, he reached out to press two fingers against her neck.

And found a steady heartbeat.

"*Draanth.*" The breath left his lungs in a rush and for a moment he felt physically weak. She was alive. Hurt, but alive.

"Come on, little human," he murmured as he pulled her free from the wreckage of the couch and into his arms. "Let's get you out of there."

Dropping back to the bed on his ass, he cradled her close and closed his eyes. They were on a remote planet, with a crashed ship, without food or water, but he didn't care. All that mattered was the small woman in his arms still drew breath.

Leaning forward, he placed a gentle kiss atop her hair, remaining there for a moment to breathe in her smell. He'd always wondered what her hair smelled like, how it felt, but she'd never let him get close enough before.

It held hints of herris blossoms... he smiled. The flowers were tiny and delicate, so feminine that he was surprised his warrior-like mate had chosen their scent. But it suited her. Despite the fragile appearance of their flowers, herris trees were strong and steadfast, capable of weathering any storm or drought. Just like his Jane.

She murmured and he eased up his grip, letting her head roll back against his arm so he could see her face. Her eyes fluttered open, unfocused and dark at first, then latched onto him with effort. Awake, but groggy, he realized.

"Hey, beautiful." He smiled. "About time you woke up."

"Hi," she said, her voice so low he wasn't sure he'd heard it. She swallowed, and winced. "How long was I asleep?"

"Only a little while." He shrugged one shoulder, careful not to jostle her, and reached up to smooth a lock of her cropped hair back. It wasn't out of place, but he needed to touch her. "You bumped your head and needed the rest."

Her speech seemed fine, and her pupils were the same size, not showing any signs of cerebral damage. She hadn't moved other than to burrow closer to him, as though desperate for his body heat. The small shiver she gave assured him he was right. She was cold.

Reaching around, he grabbed for the bedcovers. They were *eedireen* so the temperature would need to be colder than deep space for them to freeze.

"That makes sense. Is that why I can't remember my name?"

He froze, arm half twisted around behind him. "What did you say?"

Her gaze was level on his when he looked back at her. But despite her calm exterior, he could see a hint of panic and vulnerability in her eyes.

"I can't remember who I am." She bit her lip, searching his face as though looking for the answers she needed.

"Do you remember me?" His voice was careful. Pulling the blanket around with one hand, he shook the snow free and wrapped it around her.

"No..." she admitted softly, eyelids fluttering

closed for a moment as she nestled into the new warmth of the blanket. "But for some reason I trust you, and something tells me I don't trust many people."

He almost smiled at that. Even without her memory she was a strong woman, and intelligent. She knew things about herself, about her personality, even if she couldn't remember why. Perhaps because of the military training she'd had.

But one thing was evident. The harder mask had been stripped away to reveal the woman she'd been concealing within. One he'd only caught glimpses of and very much wanted to get to know more without her shields set at maximum.

"No, you don't trust many." He paused for a moment, trying to fight temptation, but lost. "You do trust me. My name is Karryl; I'm your mate."

Surprise flowed across her face for a second. "Mate? Like...married?"

Karryl nodded, pulling her closer. "Yes, little mate. Married. We're married and it's my job to look after you. Protect you."

He sighed when she murmured happily and settled closer to him.

It wasn't a lie. Not really, she'd have accepted his claim...eventually.

He'd just hastened things along a little.

JANE. Her name was Jane.

The blanket wrapped around her shoulders, she huddled by a small fire in front of the crashed shuttle. The name meant as much to her as the word tree or mountain. She couldn't make it connect in the blank fog that was her memory. But she remembered other things. Like the sound of rain on the windows, and the unbearable heat of late summer in the city. She remembered playing as a child on a crowded sidewalk beside towering apartment buildings and looking at the sky, wondering what was out there. And she remembered the utter silence of space as she'd looked on her home planet from orbit for the first time. She knew that while this wasn't earth, she was human.

And the man who sat on the other side of the fire wasn't.

Tall, broad shouldered and clad entirely in leather, he was hot whatever species he was. With a capital H-O-T. Long dark hair cascaded over his shoulders as he concentrated on the device he was trying to fix, his unusual, cat-slitted eyes narrowed. Even without access to her memories, she knew he was the sexiest man she'd ever slapped eyes on. She watched him boldly, not bothering to conceal her curiosity.

My name is Karryl, I'm your mate.

Mr. Hotty was her husband. Holy hell, how had she gotten so lucky? He was obviously strong and capable, clearing the snow from inside the shuttle and covering the broken view screen so the interior was weatherproof. The fire was likewise his handiwork, and now he was fiddling with the electronics in the box on his lap with an expertise that spoke of intelligence.

As though he sensed her attention, he looked up and smiled. The expression took his cruelly handsome features into panty-wetting gorgeous, those turquoise and violet eyes twinkling. She blushed and looked down, only to glance up again a moment later to check him out. He still watched her, but the smile had gone, replaced by a raw hunger that took her breath away.

He held her gaze for a moment, then looked down, his lips quirking as a braid of his hair fell forward.

All that heat directed at her... she swallowed,

barely containing the little moan that wanted to escape her lips. They were married. That meant they'd had sex. Hell, if he looked at her like that a lot, like he wanted to eat her alive, she'd be surprised if they were ever out of bed.

Clearing her throat, she asked. "How long have we been..."

He flicked a glance up, spearing her with a direct look. "Mated?"

"Yeah. Married, mated, whatever you want to call it."

Mated sounded weird but struck a chord deep within her. It felt right, the idea that they were a couple. Like they'd been made for each other. Figured, her perfect man would be alien. Probably all the years in the...she almost caught it, but the thought slithered away like an eel. Dammit.

"Not long. Only a couple weeks."

He pushed some loose wires back into place and put the cover on the box he'd been working on and screwed it down. Some kind of rescue beacon, apparently. His lips curved into a little smile, a dimple playing peekaboo in one cheek. "We would have been mated sooner, but you made me chase you."

"Really?" She couldn't keep the surprise out of her voice. "What, with the way you I—"

Crap. She cut the sentence off before she embarrassed herself further, heat crawling over her cheeks.

"No, no. What were you going to say?" he asked, elbows resting on his knees and the beacon held loosely in large hands. She'd always loved men's hands and his were beautiful. Strong and well formed. "The way I what?"

"You're fishing for compliments. I'm surprised I led you on a chase with the way...well, look at you." She waved her hand in his general direction. "You're drop-dead gorgeous, ripped as hell and intelligent to boot. What's not for any woman to like?"

He looked stunned for a moment, then a shit-eating grin worthy of any smug testosterone-fueled grunt spread over his face. "You think I'm gorgeous?"

"Oh, get over yourself. I married you, didn't I?" She chuckled and snuggled into the warmth of her blankets. "I really should be helping you with all this. I'm not helpless, it was only a little bump on the head."

"Not a chance, little human," he shot back, expression firm. "That little bump, as you call it, has caused enough problems already. You're not making it worse by overexerting yourself. You need to rest."

He stood, flipping a switch on the beacon. It chirped, green lights flickering to life on the front panel.

"Success?" she asked, sitting up a little.

The movement of the blankets caused a gap around her neck, and the cold was quick to reach icy fingers within. With the shuttle behind them trashed beyond repair, the beacon was their only way off this ice-ridden planet.

"Indeed," he smiled over his shoulder as he turned to fit the beacon into a bracket attached to a tripod, its feet buried beneath the compacted snow. The muscles in his back and shoulders worked as he winched it higher. Jane's attention wandered down, admiring the width of his shoulders, the lean waist, and trim hip. And his ass...

"Like what you see?"

His amused comment made her snap her gaze up. He wasn't even looking at her, his back still turned. She frowned.

"What makes you think I'm looking at you?"

He chuckled, the deep rich sound stroking along her senses, like he'd touched her himself. "Little human, I can always tell when you're looking at me. It pleases me that you like my body."

Liked his body? Hell yeah, she liked it. More than liked it, but she didn't say that, shaking her head instead. "Yeah, well, get over yourself. Once you've seen one guy with his kit off, you've seen them all."

He dropped in front of her, faster than anyone had a right to move, and she squeaked. His strange eyes flashed with fire. "You won't be seeing any other males without their clothes, ever again. You're mine, Jane, now and forever."

8

*J*ane had always been beautiful, but every time Karryl had seen her, she'd been guarded. A whirlwind of driven purpose and energy with her shields set so high, no man could hope to breach them. No doubt a result of all her years as a soldier and he could see her aboard one of the Earth vessels, bellowing orders.

He'd seen her in action a few times. A deadly beauty with an assault rifle and an aim that put half his men to shame; she was all hard edges and lethality. A package designed to make even a holy man give up his vows on the spot. Whatever else Karryl was, he sure as hell wasn't a holy man.

He'd always wondered what lay beyond the hardness. Her circumstances and life had shaped her into a warrior, but he wanted the woman. He'd seen the occasional glimpse, like when she'd dropped her guard with her friends and forgot to be the hard-ass soldier, but the walls went back up before he could see more. But those glimpses made him ache to discover more. He wondered what she looked like when she relaxed totally. When she didn't think anyone was watching her, when she forgot to be the "Marine major" her people spoke about with such awe and was just...Jane.

Now he knew. Without her memory, the harder edges had fallen away. She was still confident, self-assured, and had retained the sharp wit that delighted him, but she was softer. Her movements were more feminine and graceful. As though in an attempt to fit into a man's world, she'd suppressed some of what made her a woman and now she didn't have to.

It was fascinating, and alluring at the same time. Especially the way she kept flicking him little glances from under her lashes as she moved around the now dry and warm interior of the shuttle. He'd cleared it out and secured the broken screen, so even though a snowstorm raged outside, they were safe within.

Though the engines were trashed and power in

the shuttle was offline, he'd managed to string power cells together into a makeshift heating unit and had melted snow for them to wash in. She'd taken hers into the little washroom at the back of the cabin for privacy but since the door was broken off, used in the view screen repair, he'd snuck a look anyway. Even though his back was supposed to be turned.

Naked to the waist, he stretched out on the bed, putting his hands behind his head. When he spotted her watching, he clenched his abdomen. Showing off maybe, but he liked the look in her eyes when she looked at him.

She liked to watch, he'd discovered, and those little glances, full of heat and need, set his blood on fire. Already painfully hard, his cock strained against his leathers. Watching her watching him just made it worse.

She was a funny little thing, full of idiosyncrasies he hadn't realized. Like her habit of humming softly under her breath as she moved. Little tunes without words that soothed something feral within him. She was shy around him. Not skittish, she was too confident in herself for that, but the high flush on her cheeks as she disrobed to sleep suited her. Made him ache to wrap her in his arms and protect her.

"Come to bed, little human," he urged, patting the soft surface beside him.

Her gaze flicked to the bed, and he held his breath, waiting for her to come to him. She did, sitting on the side of the sleeping mat then swinging her legs up to lie down. Avoiding his eyes, she wriggled a little closer. He hid his smile and pulled her in, settling her against him with a contented sigh. So many nights he'd dreamed of her lying next to him, sleeping safely wrapped in his arms. If he was honest, although his body burned for hers, it was the closeness, having a mate of his own, that his soul craved.

He planted a soft kiss on the top of her head and relaxed, closing his eyes. His cock throbbed in frustration, but he ignored it. Now was not the time and place. Jane was injured, and he wouldn't risk his little mate, not even to ease his frustrated passions.

They were safe, for now, and warm. The emergency beacon was transmitting on a frequency only the Lathar were aware of, so rescue should be on its way. They couldn't be far off the main space lanes, so it shouldn't take long. Hopefully a couple of days, long enough for him to seduce his way far enough into Jane's heart that when she recovered her memory, she couldn't reject him.

Her hand whispered over his chest, the movement more than accidental. He looked down to find her looking up at him.

"My love?" The endearment was startled from him, but at the sudden warm look in her eyes, he refused to take it back.

"So, we're married..." She trailed her fingertips in little patterns over the width of his chest. Never had he been so aware of the skin there as she brushed it gently with soft fingers. Unbidden his arm tightened around her waist.

"Yes, we are." His answer was automatic, all his senses focused on her. A herd of *kervasi* could have rampaged through the cabin and he wouldn't have paid any attention.

"I can't..." she paused, as though searching for the words, and her indecision, the little wrinkle of her nose, made him want to kiss her all the more.

"I can't remember us...being together." Her eyes, wide and dark, lifted to his in entreaty. "Help me remember?"

Fuck. The breath punched from Karryl's lungs as he realized what she was asking, what she wanted. She wanted them to... His body reacted instantly, back to painfully hard from the half state of arousal he always found himself in around her.

"Are you sure, little human?"

He heard himself say the words as he shifted on the bed, taking her with him so he leaned over her, protective and possessive. The memory of their brief encounter on the outpost, on this same bed, surged to the front. Inflamed his arousal. She was so tiny compared to him, and that fired his blood even more.

"You are injured, it might—" he ducked his head, hardly believing what he was saying. Looked up at her through the veil of his hair. "I would never forgive myself if my taking you caused you pain."

Her lips curved into a soft smile and she reached up to thread her fingers through the fall of his hair, smoothing it back in a loving gesture that hit him right in the middle of his chest.

"I might not be able to remember much about my past, just fragments here and there, but I'm sure I'm not the sort of woman to cry over a broken fingernail. Correct?"

His chuckle was soft, rueful, and he nodded. "Yes, my love. You're a strong woman. Independent and capable. It's what drew me to you."

Her fingers were still tangled in his hair, curling around the nape of his neck to pull his head down. Her words were soft puffs of air over his lips. "I won't break, I promise. Help me remember us...me and you. Love me."

He closed his eyes for a moment, trying to find the strength to refuse. The pull to take what she offered beat at him, but she didn't remember...yet how could he refuse such a gently-worded plea?

Her mouth over his ended his mental debate. She kissed him softly, hands in his hair as she pulled him to her. It would be okay, they were headed here anyway, he told himself, they would have mated back on the outpost had the Krynassis not interrupted them.

With a groan, he gave into her invitation and wrapped her up in his arms. His tongue sweeping the closed seam of her mouth, he demanded entry and growled softly when she granted it with a soft moan.

She was pliant and willing, and nothing would stop him making her his.

HEAVENS, Karryl kissed like a sex god. No wonder she'd married him.

Jane moaned as he slid one arm beneath her neck, the other around her waist as he pushed a leather-clad leg between hers. He surrounded her, above and around her as his tongue invaded her mouth. Slid and stroked hers in demand and temptation. The need that had been simmering all day flared into life. His kiss was full of wicked mischief and pure alpha dominance, a contradiction that confused her and kept her coming back for more.

Her moans were lost under kiss after kiss. He alternated open-mouthed, hot as hell kisses with long, drugging ones that left her breathing ragged and her heart racing. She squirmed against him, riding his thigh. Heat flooded her cheeks when she realized she was practically dry-humping his leg.

Hands splayed out over his broad chest, she reveled in the hard muscles and satin skin. She brushed her fingertips over his nipple and he jerked. A low hiss escaped his lips as she kissed along his jaw at the same time her hands smoothed down his body.

She teased along his waistband, dipping beneath the leather to stroke the satin skin. Each time she did, his stomach tensed and clenched to drive his hips against her. She reached for his belt buckle, but before she could undo it, his hand covered hers.

"No," his lips quirked into a wicked grin. "My turn."

Within a half second, she found both her hands pinned above her head by one of his. He moved over her, kissing the side of her neck as his free hand yanked her top loose of her pants. A whimper slid from her as his big, rough hand smoothed over her skin, moving upward to cover her breast.

He paused, breath hot on her throat as he encountered no barriers. She wore nothing beneath, soft skin and sensitive nipples open to his touch. A deep groan whispered against her skin. He dipped his tongue into the gap at the base of her throat between her collarbones, rolling her nipple between his thumb and forefinger. Sharp pleasure arrowed through her and she arched her back, offering more of herself to him.

A deep ache filled her. An ache for him and only him. For him to touch her, stroke her, tease her, and then bring her the kinds of pleasure she'd only dreamed of. She knew he could, the knowledge was there every time he looked at her. In every touch, every little look. The heat that flared every time he looked at her. There was a fire in her blood with only one remedy: his cock buried so deeply inside her she didn't know where he ended and she began.

"Please..." she begged, moving restlessly against him.

"Soon, my love." His words were a caress against her skin. He pushed her top up, letting go of her hands to pull the garment clear. She tried to touch him, but he stopped her, pushing her hands up and placing them against the wall.

"Don't move them," he ordered, eyes blazing with command. She swallowed, a thrill shooting through her. Hunched over her as he was, he looked dark and dangerous, a feral god about to consume the offering laid out for him.

Her.

Her clit throbbed in agreement with that plan. She bit her lip, leaving her hands where he'd placed them as he moved down over her body. His breath curled around her nipple a second before the wet rasp of his tongue flicked over it. The peak beaded into a hard point as if begging for more, a message he read easily. His tongue laved over her and around the sensitive nipple. His big hand cupped and caressed her, plumping and molding the slight mound and holding her in place for his mouth. She held her breath as he hovered over the peak.

Closing his lips around her, he pulled her into the wet heat of his mouth and sucked. Her low moan was liquid with pleasure as sensation shot through her, her clit aching in response. She couldn't help moving restlessly against him. She needed more, of everything. Of his touch. His kiss. Everything. Her hands moved on the metal of the bulkhead, one losing contact and almost reaching down for him.

His hand shot out, slamming hers back into place and covering it. "I told you not to move, little human. Do as you're told or suffer the consequences."

His rough tone made her whimper, but not as much as when he moved farther down. His lips flirted with the soft curves of her stomach. He kissed the soft skin, hands urgent on her pants. Any finesse was gone now as he tore at the fastenings. She lifted her hips to help him slide them and her panties over her hips. In an instant, they were gone and she was naked before him.

Chills chased over her skin as he sat back on his heels, eyes dark as he swept his gaze over her body. A flush spread over her cheeks as he looked his fill, as though he'd never seen a woman before. Never seen her before. But that was madness. They were married so he'd seen her naked before. He'd seen everything about her...had to have.

"You're beautiful," he said roughly, reaching out

to wrap a big hand around her ankle. "So beautiful you take my breath away every time I look at you."

Emotion filled her and she made to move, but the warning flash in his eyes made her put her hands back. His dominance frustrated and thrilled her. She wanted to disobey, just to see what he'd do, but something about him warned her against it. Like he needed her this way at the moment, needed to look and touch without her touching him.

Slowly, he pulled her legs apart, gaze devouring the sight of her body opening for him. She kept silent, watched his face tighten in need as her pussy was revealed. He crawled forward, the power and strength in his body evident. Heavily carved muscles moved smoothly as he shouldered her legs apart and settled between them.

She had to close her eyes, the erotic sight of him between her spread thighs, too much for her. He'd seemed big before, clad in his warrior's leathers, but now...

He blew a soft breath over her and her clit throbbed in response. All thought processes scrambled as he leaned forward to run his tongue over her pussy lips. The warm, wet brush made her jump, then melt. With a small grunt of approval, he wrapped big hands around her hips, holding her still for him as he found her clit and latched onto it.

He sucked and she was lost. Soft moans and whimpers filled the air around them, her body arching and writhing at his sensual attack. He gave no quarter, driving her higher and higher without mercy. Just when she thought she couldn't take any more, he pulled back. She sagged against the sheets, but he wasn't done with her yet. Two strong fingers teased the entrance to her core. She tensed, all attention on him. She felt his smile against her lower lips and the tiny flicker of his tongue, then he thrust the digits deep into her needy pussy.

The scream escaped her before she could stop it, her release crashing down over her without warning. Her hips rocked, riding his hand and mouth as he guided her pleasure and drew out her release, each wave stealing her ability to form a coherent thought.

Finally, they died away a little and he released her, stripping his clothes and crawling over her with predatory intent written into every line of his body. His face was tight, handsome and cruel at the same time. The banked fire she'd seen in his eyes earlier was in full flame now and the intensity of it scorching. She caught her breath, knowing that no matter how many times they'd been together in the past, *this* was the one that mattered. This time would brand him on her very soul.

"Mine," he murmured, gripping her behind the knee and holding her leg high against his hip. The thick head of his cock nudged at her entrance and she swallowed. He was huge. Enormous. But they'd done this before, she reminded herself, so it had to work. Really had to work.

She brushed her fingers along his jaw and smiled. Tried to smile. Her breathing caught halfway when he pushed forward and her smile became a gasp.

Holding himself above her, he watched her expression as he pressed in. His cock split her, her pussy parting around him, stretching to accommodate his girth. Forgetting his instruction to keep her hands on the wall, she clutched at his muscled upper arms. Bracing and holding herself still as his cock slid deeper.

Her lips parted into a small *O*. His possession was pleasure and almost-pain, her body burning even as it accepted him. Stopping the forward motion, he pulled back, giving her a moment's reprieve, then pushed in again. Each back and forward motion was easier, until finally, he was in her to the hilt.

He gripped the back of her neck, holding her still so he could look into her eyes. His expression was full of fire and concern. For her. The little pause melted her heart even more. No words passed between them; none needed. The fire in her pussy eased, leaving her with a sense of anticipation, and she nodded.

The muscles in his forearm bunched as he moved. He held her close, pulling back to drive back into her. The first hard thrust, eased by the juices of her own arousal, stole her breath. The second scattered her ability to think. By the third, she was screaming his name, her nails digging into his shoulders as he took her over and over again. She locked her gaze with his, unable to look away. Each drive, each time his hips met hers, felt like he was claiming her.

"Mine, always mine," he said, his grip tightening on the back of her neck. Not tight enough to hurt, but firm. "Say it, Jane. Say you're mine."

"Yours, always yours," she whispered and shattered again, her body convulsing around his cock buried deeply within. His expression tightened and then it was as if her release opened the floodgates to his.

With a growl, he pulled her to him, his thrusts harder and faster as she came. Within a few thrusts he stiffened, throwing his head back to roar his release as he spilled his seed within her silken walls.

9

*T*he planet they'd crashed on was beautiful.

Early the next morning, Jane stood outside the shuttle, bucket in hand, and stood to take in the view. Mountains rose on either side, majestic peaks covered with glittering white snow. High cliffs decorated the pale vista with slices of lavender blue. The sky was cerulean, without a cloud in sight, and the heat of the twin suns overhead made even the icy temperatures feel bearable.

With a contented sigh, she trudged through the snow. The leather pants and boots she wore, similar to Karryl's, shrugged off the icy white particles trying to cling to her. Just a little way up the rise, she decided, and there would be enough clean, fresh snow for her to melt over the fire for coffee.

"Don't go too far. There are predators on this planet." Karryl's voice sounded behind her, the familiar, deep tones sparking a rush of emotion within her.

With a smile, she turned and looked over her shoulder. "Oh, I'm aware of that. I'm looking at the biggest one out there."

"Then you need to be doubly careful, don't you?" His answering grin set a fire burning within her veins again.

Falling asleep just before the dual sunrise, they'd slept in late after a night of passion that would be etched in her memory forever. He had been insatiable, letting her rest only for a little while before waking her again in a variety of sensual and erotic ways to take her again. If this was married life, then why the hell had she waited so long to get married?

"A delectable little morsel like you could get snapped up, just like that." He moved quicker than any man that big should, powerful thighs driving him through the snow as he launched himself towards her.

With a delighted squeal, she dropped the bucket

and ran. She didn't have his power, though, and the knee-high snow hampered her progress. Her heart pounded in her chest, thrills running through her as he closed in. She dodged and weaved, but it was no good. Within seconds his arms wrapped around her, spinning her around, hauling her into his embrace.

"Look what I've caught," his lips, surprisingly full in such a masculine face, curved into a wicked little smile. She wrapped her fingers in the lapels of his jacket as he bent his head. His lips grazed hers, and she parted them in anticipation...

Sssswwwhoooosssshhhh...

The loud sound overhead had them both looking up. A streak of blue-white fire across the sky announced the arrival of another shuttle.

"The beacon worked! They've found us!" She gasped, hugging him in delight.

Karryl didn't seem as impressed or happy about the imminent rescue as she was. His body tight with tension, his expression was set as he watched the shuttle execute a lazy loop to head back to them.

"Go back to the shuttle," he ordered. "Put the gray robes on, and pull the hood up. Don't come out unless I tell you to."

She opened her mouth to argue, but paused and frowned. A chill of unease crept along her spine.

With or without her memories, he didn't strike her as the panicking type. If he was worried, then there was something to be worried about.

"Go. Now. Run, before they see you." He gave a little push in the direction of the shuttle. It didn't take her long to reach it, lifting her knees high to clear the snow as she ran. Reaching the shuttle door, she dove inside, casting a prayer of thanks to the woman she had been. She might not be curvy, or appear particularly feminine, but she was obviously serious about fitness.

Once inside she grabbed the gray robes and hauled them on. Pulling the hood up to conceal her face, she peeked out the door.

The shuttle had landed, door on the side open, and three warriors stood in front of Karryl. Even from this distance, it was obvious he was bigger and more heavily muscled than any of them. They wore leather as he did, and sashes across their chests. One red, two gold. A memory surfaced of Karryl wearing a similar gold sash, his expression heated and frustrated...full of anger as he looked down at her. Deliberately, she didn't try to hold onto it, knowing it would slip away as soon as she did, and the scene filled out.

They were in a corridor. He was angry with her. She didn't want him to leave...

The three warriors from the shuttle moved, looking past Karryl as he motioned at the shuttle. She shrank back into the shadows. He'd said to stay hidden, and since he knew more about this world at the moment than she did, she had to trust his judgement. She couldn't stay hidden forever though. Since the point of rescue was to get them both off the planet, they'd have to come clean about the fact there were two of them. Not just one.

After a few minutes conversation, Karryl turned and motioned her forward with a wave. Hesitantly, she stepped out of cover. Making sure her hood and robes secure about her, she picked her way to the group of warriors.

Karryl held his arm out for her as she reached them. She slid beneath it, her hands against his chest and side as he pulled her close. The embrace was both protective and possessive and he turned back to the others.

"This is my mate, Jane Allen of Earth."

Surprise flowed over the three men's faces. The one in the middle, who she assumed to be the leader, started a little before looking her up and down. "Really? I had not thought to be fortunate enough to meet any of the Terran women."

He smiled and offered his hand. "I am Ishaan F'Naar, my lady. A pleasure to make your acquaintance."

Something about him rose the hackles on the back of her neck. There was no way she was taking his hand. He was handsome and polite, but she didn't trust him. The idea of touching even the smallest part of him made her skin crawl. He reminded her of someone, but like all the others, she couldn't place the memory.

"You will have to excuse my mate." Karryl's arm tightened around her, his voice low with overtones of *fuck off and die*. "She is from a culture which frowns on casual touching. They keep their touch for their mates alone."

She kept her expression neutral, just in case they could see under the hood. She was pretty sure her culture wasn't like that, but if it meant she didn't have to touch Mr. Snake in the Grass, then it worked for her.

"Of course. I do apologize, I did not mean to cause offense." Ishaan inclined his head. Looking at Karryl once more, he stepped back and motioned toward the shuttle behind him. "If you and your mate are ready to leave, my ship is at your disposal."

RESCUE OR NOT, Karryl wanted to punch Ishaan F'Naar in the face. Repeatedly. With the butt of a laser rifle.

Sitting on one side of the shuttle, Jane tucked into his side, he feigned the worn-out rescuee and studied Ishaan and his men from under lowered lashes. No one would be fooled that he was resting. His body was coiled tightly, ready to retaliate should any of them make a move.

He didn't trust the F'Naar. Never had. They claimed loyalty to Daaynal, but he'd long since had his doubts about them. Neither large nor particularly skillful like the K'Vass, nor with any particularly advantageous bloodlines, they were the kind of war clan who kept their cards close to their chest and played the odds.

He hadn't been inclined to trust them before. The hairs on the back of his neck had risen as soon as he'd recognized the clan insignia on the shuttle, and the speed they'd responded to the distress call bothered him. They'd gotten here too fast, which meant they'd been in the area. An area of space no Lathar were supposed to be. An area of space where Latharian technology had been attacked with *keraton* weaponry... which the F'Naar had dabbled with in the past.

Arm around Jane, he tucked her closer to his side. *Draanth,* he really did not like her in this situation. For a moment, he wished she had all her memories. Having another experienced battle-hardened warrior at his side would be an advantage. Well, right up to the point she handed his ass to him on a plate for lying to her about them being mated.

He didn't regret that. There was no way in this lifetime he'd ever regret their night together. Taking her, feeling her delicate, strong body moving beneath his had been an experience he'd never thought he would be blessed with. She'd been soft, and sweet, clinging to him in passion in a way that fed into his male ego. Soothed and baited the primal animal within. She'd felt so right in his arms, he knew he'd never look at another female, of any species, ever again.

She was it for him.

Their joining had been... he'd never known sex could be so mind-blowing. Not just physical but spiritual as well. When they'd joined, shared release together, he felt her soul mesh to his.

At least he hoped so, because if they had bonded, the presence of mating marks on his wrist might stop her from killing him when she recovered her memory. He hadn't forgotten how lethal she was.

Amusement quirked his lips. Stars, wouldn't that confuse the F'Naar? Having their first experience of humans being a hard as nails female warrior brave enough to face down a horde of Krynassis and beat them into submission? He almost felt sorry for them. It was so far out of their realm of experience, they wouldn't know what to do with her.

It had taken him long enough to get his head around it. At first he'd bemoaned the fact she wasn't sweet and compliant like Tarrick's little Cat. He seemed to have little difficulty getting the Earth beauty into bed, whereas Karryl had to fight tooth and claw to get so much as a kiss. But now he wouldn't have her any other way. She was perfect.

Shifting position on the bench, he ran a finger beneath his wrist bracer as if to scratch an itch. Without being obvious, he lifted the edge to check underneath, hoping beyond hope that there would be black marks on the skin.

Nothing. The skin was unmarked and pale. Not

surprising. It had taken almost a week before the marks had shown up on Tarrick's skin, not less than the twelve hours it had been since he'd made Jane his. Not that mating marks would stop Ishaan and his men from trying to kill him if the F'Naar wanted to claim Jane.

This time his grin broke free. Poor bastard, Karryl didn't pity him if he tried to force the fierce little human female. He knew her, probably as well as she knew herself. She was a warrior through and through. Forced into such a situation, she'd pretend compliance, then as soon as her enemy's guard was down, she'd rip his guts out with whatever she had at hand. Slowly.

"Almost there," Ishaan leaned forward as the shuttle slowed to maneuver into the shuttle bay. A slight bump indicated touchdown.

"Zaanar here will show you to our guest quarters so you and your mate can refresh yourselves. May I assume the pleasure of your company tonight? We have an *Esatliine* chef on board. His dishes..." He closed his eyes in pleasure. "Exquisite."

Karryl's gaze flicked to the indicated warrior for a moment. "My thanks, you honor us. Now, if you don't mind, I'd like to get my mate rested."

Ishaan and the remaining warrior stepped back

with a half bow, allowing Karryl and Jane to follow Zaanar out the now opened shuttle door. Tension crawled up Karryl's spine as they walked. He didn't like having his back to heavily-armed warriors not of his clan. He'd do anything to have some of his brothers in arms around him. Hell, he'd even hug that asshole healer Laarn if he showed up.

Their footsteps, two heavy male treads and the lighter steps belonging to the woman at his side, rang in the corridor as Zaanar led them through the ship. Tall, broad-shouldered, and heavily muscled, he had dark hair shaved to the scalp at the sides, numerous warrior braids decorating the top section, pulled tightly and secured at the back. A lot of braids for such a young warrior, almost as many as Karryl himself wore. He seemed familiar for some reason, but Karryl couldn't place him. He shook off the feeling. He'd probably seen Zaanar the few occasions the F'Naar had put in at Lathar Prime.

Finally, he paused in front of a door. His hand shot out, stopping Karryl as he turned to enter the rooms.

"A warning to the wise," his voice was deeper than Karryl had expected, with a gravelly quality that pulled at his memory. "Have a care with what belongs to you." His gaze flicked to Jane as she moved silently past them and through the open door. "Some aboard this ship have eyes for what is not theirs. And to say they are not bedfellows with honor would be an understatement."

Karryl nodded, placing his hand over the other warriors. "Understood. My thanks."

Turning, he walked through the door and paused for a moment as it slid shut behind him. No way to lock it from this side, and no access panel he could hack into to secure it. *Draanth.* Not good.

A familiar female voice made him snap his head up, eyes narrowed. That sounded like Cat, Tarrick's mate... His eyes widened as he saw Jane sitting on the bed, her gaze riveted on a console in front of her. Cat Moore's face filled the screen and his heart sank.

Slowly, Jane turned around, tension in every line of her body. Her eyes lifted to meet his, the mismatched orbs cold and angry, and he knew.

Her memory was back.

JANE HAD TRIED NOT to gawk on their walk through the alien vessel. Everything seemed so big, larger-than-life, and looking at the warriors that surrounded them she could understand why. Every time she looked at Karryl, his size took her breath away. From the few memories she did have, she realized the Lathar were far bigger than humans. But she kept her thoughts to herself, walking silently at Karryl's side as they were shown to their quarters. With a sigh of relief she slid past him into the room, eager to get rid of the concealing robe. She understood why he'd wanted her to wear it. There was just something about that Ishaan F'Naar she didn't trust. Something about him that tugged at her memory, and she had a feeling that wasn't a good thing.

Leaving Karryl talking to the warrior at the door, she advanced farther into the room. It was bigger than the shuttle had been, with the same kind of molded to the floor and walls furniture. One thing she had to say for the Lathar, their technology was both functional and beautiful. She hadn't expected any kind of beauty from a race so warlike.

As though triggered by movement in the room, a screen on the wall opposite the bed flickered to life. A woman's face filled it, expression filled with concern. Jane froze, stopped in place as though she'd been poleaxed. She knew that face...

"Jane? It's Cat. If you get this, we just wanted you to know we're worried about you... That we're all worried about you," the woman leaned forward, eyes intent. "Even the emperor, Daaynal, is concerned. There have been... developments at home. No one will talk to me, Commodore Fuller just keeps asking for you. Apparently, I don't have the correct *clearances*. Please, wherever you are... You need to get in contact with us. Sergeant Cat Moore, over and out."

Jane closed her eyes as memory hit. It returned hard and fast, slamming into her like a barrage of hollow point bullets. Cat. Earth. Fuller... *Oh shit.*

Her eyes snapped open. That asshole Fuller demanded information from her or he was arming the nukes. There was still so much they didn't understand about the Lathar, but she couldn't imagine that would be good. Just like she couldn't imagine they wouldn't know. Their technology was so much more advanced than humanity's, there was no way they would miss a little thing like nukes being armed. No way in hell. She dreaded to think what their likely reaction would be.

More memories crowded in, one after the other until she thought her head would explode. The attack on the base, her trying to hold the central section, the big warrior and his men who'd attacked them. Her gasp echoed the sliding of the door as it closed, and slowly she turned to look at the man standing framed in front of it.

Karryl K'Vass. One of the aliens who had captured the base, kidnapped her and the rest of the women aboard. The alien warrior who'd been trying to claim her as his mate since. The sexy alien she hadn't been able to get out of her mind from the moment she'd seen him. The man she'd almost given herself to on the outpost, ready to agree to whatever he wanted just so he'd carry on kissing her. The man she'd trusted on the planet, when she couldn't remember anything.

He'd told her they were married...

"You fucking asshole." Rage burned within her as she rose slowly to her feet, body tight, ready to attack. She didn't give a damn about the beauty of the room anymore, or the fact her home planet might have made a decision that would get it blown out of space. Her attention was solely focused on the man in front of her. "You fucking lied to me. Why?"

He stepped forward, hands out in the universal gesture of surrender. "Jane, please..."

"Don't you fucking please me, you—"

"Yeah, lying asshole, I get it. You're mad at me."

For a scary as hell alien warrior, Karryl did a damn good impression of a penitent man. The trouble was, she wasn't impressed, and right at that moment, didn't believe a word that came out of the man's mouth. Her brain chose that moment to remind her just how talented he was with his mouth, and his lips...and his tongue. Heat simmered through her, a shiver washing over her skin as he stalked closer.

He must have caught the little movement because his expression changed between one heartbeat and the next. She wanted to hit him and kiss him at the same time. What the fuck was wrong with her?

"Mad?" She barked out a laugh. "You lie to me, use memory loss to get me into your bed...what do you fucking think?"

He stopped within a step of her. She refused to back down, her head tilted to glare up at him. Awareness shot through her, holding her as the tension built between them. His expression was hard, features drawn tightly as he looked down at her. Her pussy clenched, liquid heat slipping from her to dampen her panties.

His nostrils flared and her cheeks burned. Shit, could he smell her excitement? She hoped not. Sure, his hard-edged warrior thing might make her hot, but he was still a fucking asshole and she didn't want to jump his bones. Not really. Well, maybe a little... but sex wouldn't solve the issues between them.

"What do I think?" He moved without warning, hard hand wrapping around the back of her neck. She gasped at the contact, the sound cut off when he hauled her up against him. "I think you needed an excuse to admit you wanted me."

"What!? Of all the egotistical, misogynistic fucking twaddle!"

Fury overwhelmed her arousal. Winding her arm back, she punched him in the shoulder. Hard. The blow rocked him on his feet for a moment, but he held fast. Lips compressing, he grabbed for her wrist and they wrestled for a moment. It didn't last long, his strength far superior to hers. Within seconds, he captured her hand, twisting it up her back. Not hard enough to hurt but enough to immobilize.

"Last night you came to me, little human. Begged me to take you..."

Shit. She had. Her cheeks went from warm to supernova in a nano-second. "Because you lied, remember?"

She hit him with her free hand, the blow glancing off his other shoulder. A warning. She couldn't get enough room for a proper blow to the face. At least that's what she told herself. "Let me go, asshole."

He increased pressure on her pinned wrist, making her gasp. His lips hovered tantalizingly above hers, mere millimeters away. "I will, on one condition."

She paused as everything within her went still. What game was he playing now? "What?"

"Prove you don't want me. Kiss me."

10

*J*ane snarled, fighting Karryl's hold, but it was no good. He held her easily, absorbing her struggles with his larger body. His larger, very hard, very...aroused body. The thick bar of his cock pressed into her stomach, making her knees weak and her resolve waver.

Oh, screw him. He wanted a kiss, so she'd give him a damn kiss. Then she'd walk away, feathers totally unruffled and show him just who had control of this situation.

Rising on her toes as much as his grip would allow, she pressed her lips to his and kissed him hard, taking no prisoners. There, she could do this... She could so do this. Who did he think he was messing with? Some wet-behind-the-ears young girl with a crush? Hell no, she was a battle-hardened marine, a mature woman who knew exactly what she wanted, when she wanted it, and how she wanted it.

Then his lips softened under hers and she felt the world tilt on its axis. With a groan, she couldn't resist the urge to feather the tip of her tongue over that parting. Then within. As soon as her tongue tangled with his, she was lost. A bolt of white-hot desire raced through her, making her body sing as she crowded closer. She needed to touch him. Feel his body against hers again. His skin sliding over hers as he drove deep within...

"Bastard," she broke the kiss to pant.

Her free hand drove into his hair to pull him down for another almost punishingly hard kiss. This time, when they came up for air, their breathing was ragged and the fire in her blood demanded more. Screw it, they'd already done it so what was one more time. Just one. Then she'd tell him it was over. For good. Done and dusted. But just one more time wouldn't hurt, right?

"How about we get naked and you show me a good time, soldier?"

He pulled back a little, his expression quizzical, but the heat in his eyes and the surge of his hips against hers left no doubt as to how he felt. "I'm a warrior, not a soldier."

She shrugged. "Tom*a*toes, tom*a*rtoes. You want to argue semantics or do you want to screw?"

His eyes flashed and he grabbed her knee, hauling her leg up to press the hard cock still constrained by his pants against her pussy. "What do you think, little human?"

His lips crashed down over hers, tongue thrusting within as he rocked against her. The pressure right where she needed it and the darkly sensual invasion left her lightheaded. By the time he lifted his head, she'd forgotten where she was and whimpered in need at the loss of his touch. "Like that? You think you can take on this warrior?"

Oh god, yes. All night, for a week. She'd never felt so horny, like she hadn't had sex for years, never mind only last night. Sliding her hands down his body, she gave him a sultry look from under her lashes. "I'll eat you for breakfast, handsome. Bring it on."

His lips quirked, dark amusement flashing in his eyes for a moment before swallowed by heat. Without speaking, he lifted her, strong hands on the backs of her thighs. Her legs automatically wrapped around his waist as he walked her backward.

This time when he kissed her, he took charge. He didn't just kiss, he stormed in and claimed ownership, branding her with his touch. Her back hit the wall, her little gasp lost as he made love to her with his mouth, demanding her response. Every wicked thought and erotic need was written in the touch of his lips on hers, sweeping away all her resistance.

He dropped her legs abruptly. There was nothing gentle about him as he placed a hand in the center of her stomach to hold her in place as he tore at the fastenings on her pants.

"Off," he growled in warning. "Now. Or I'll rip them off."

Aching with need, she shoved her pants over her hips and dropped them to the floor. He unfastened his leather bindings to free himself, barely giving her time to pull off her boots before he crowded her against the wall. A hard grip behind her knee pulled her leg up his hip again.

She lost her balance, clutching at his shoulders for support. The broad head of his cock pressed against the entrance to her body and she moaned. Her pussy clenched, clit aching as she bathed him in a rush of liquid heat that dragged a deep groan from his throat.

"*Draanth,* you're already wet for me." He pushed in as he spoke, driving the steel-like thickness of his cock deep into her needy pussy. "You like this, little human, admit it."

She couldn't speak, her hands spread wide on his chest. Held off balance, with his cock pulsing deeply inside her; she was completely at his mercy. And he knew it. His lips quirked into a dark smile. "You might hate me, but you like my cock buried in your cunt, don't you?"

She couldn't answer, all her cognitive processes taken up by processing the sensations coursing through her body. He pulled out and thrust in again. Hard. Fast. Ruthless. There was no softness in the way he took her, fucking her like he hated her. Like she hated him. Raw power bent to one purpose. Pleasure or punishment, she wasn't sure which.

They moved together, straining against each other. The sounds of sex filled the room; the slap of skin on skin, wet sounds as her body clenched around his invading cock... She bit her lip, trying to keep silent, but he saw.

"No. I want to hear," he ordered on a hard thrust, pausing with his cock balls deeply inside her. "Those moans belong to me, and I'll fuck them out of you if I have to."

At the end of the thrust, he rocked, trapping her clit between them. Pleasure exploded through her and she whimpered. He did it again, then again, until she was panting with need, shaking with holding the sounds of her pleasure within. A battle of wills she was determined to win.

He moved to kiss her but she turned her head. She couldn't, not with him buried inside. The way he kissed, if he got his tongue inside her as well, she'd lose focus. Lose the battle. His lips landed on her neck and she realized her mistake. With a soft sound of pleasure, he nuzzled the soft spot beneath her ear. The one that made her weak and prepared to do anything he wanted.

"Bastard," she gasped, losing the battle against herself, temptation, and him.

"Always, just for you, and you like it, don't you?" He nipped her earlobe and she groaned, turning toward him.

Their kiss was open-mouthed and hot. Each slide of his tongue was accompanied by a hard jerk of his hips, a two-punch combination cracked her defenses. A small moan escaped, quickly stifled.

"No. More," he ordered his voice a dark temptation. "Surrender. Give yourself to me, you know you want to."

She whimpered as he pinned her hands above her head with one of his. Stretched her out as he used his body to pleasure her. Her defenses against him, already broken, started to crumble and fall. He surged forward, upward. His arm was hard around the back of her waist as he held them away from the wall. He thrust his tongue deeply. Made sweet love to her mouth even as he ravaged her body.

Her sigh of surrender was lost, but she knew he heard it. A growl of triumph rolled from deep in his chest and he renewed his efforts. With each slide of his cock within her, pleasure grew and coiled on itself until she didn't know which way was up. Giving herself over to him, she became a creature of reaction. Rode his cock as he impaled her over and over and until...

Time paused. The moment between one second and the next stretching out until it seemed infinite. Pleasure and anticipation coursed through her as she gazed into the face of the abyss and saw ecstasy staring back.

He thrust and the moment broke. Pleasure exploded through her with the force of a nuclear blast. She screamed. Something. His name. She didn't know. All she knew was she never wanted the feeling to stop.

He increased speed, hips slamming into hers as he chased his own release. Rough. Powerful. But she didn't care. Each movement stroked nerve endings she didn't know existed and spiraled her pleasure out of control.

Finally, he stiffened, throwing his head back and the cords standing out in his neck as he reached release. His groan of pleasure was music to her ears and she wrapped her now free arms around his shoulders, stroking the back of his neck as they both came down from the heights of pleasure.

He was a damn liar, but hell did he fuck like a god. Perhaps this thing would work after all...

"REMEMBER, keep the hood up and make sure the robe stays closed."

Karryl's voice was firm as he fussed about her, pulling the silver-gray robe this way and that until he was satisfied no part of her could be seen. He was the most worried she'd ever seen him, the raw and primal lover giving way to the professional soldier... warrior, whatever he wanted to call himself.

"Honestly, I can handle this." She took a step back and rolled her shoulders, easing the stiffness across the base of her neck. An old injury from the colony wars, it flared up from time to time but wasn't anything she couldn't handle.

Her words didn't seem to reassure Karryl, the big warrior checking his weaponry again. He was less armed than when they'd arrived, two of his knives and a pulse blaster now concealed under Jane's voluminous robes.

"*Draanth!*" He ran a shaking hand through his hair, his agitation clear to see. "These males...they're not honorable. I don't like this at all."

"Worry wart," she teased him with a small smile. Then her expression dropped serious as she looked directly at him. "Karryl, I survived a decade in one of the most vicious wars my kind has ever known. This isn't my first rodeo, and it won't be my last."

He paused, eyes narrowed and then shook his head at her words. "Half the time I have no clue what you're talking about."

She chuckled. "Rodeo? It's a terran thing with horses. What I mean is this is not the first time I've walked into a dangerous situation with no backup. You know what humans say about the female of the species?"

His eyebrow raised a fraction. "No. What?"

She winked and pulled up the hood as the door

chimes announced their escort. "We're more deadly than the male."

There was no more time for talking. Karryl strode to the door and opened it to reveal Zaanar and two other warriors waiting on the other side. She paused a moment as she looked at the F'Naar warrior. She had the strangest feeling that she'd seen him somewhere before.

"Lord Ishaan awaits the pleasure of your company," he announced with a bow and she couldn't shake a nagging sense of familiarity. It wasn't so much the way he looked, but something about the way he moved that struck a chord within her.

Odd. She shook off the feeling to move silently to Karryl's side. Her combat boots were well worn and she'd long since developed the ability to walk quietly when needed—¬an essential survival skill for any soldier whatever the species.

"Thank you," Kaaryl turned and extended his arm to her. "Come along, my love."

She reached out to take his arm, sliding her hand onto the leather in a gentle touch. Zaanar's gaze flicked to her and for a moment she saw a flicker of curiosity. That was to be expected. Most of these men hadn't seen a female of their own species since childhood, and by now, the rumors had to have circulated that humanity was a smaller version of the Lathar. She was going to feel like a goldfish all night.

They were led in silence through the corridors of the ship. From within the all-concealing hood, Jane missed nothing. Mentally, she noted the layout of the vessel. It was a lot smaller than the K'Vass flagship, or even the T'Laat battle-cruiser. Perhaps an indication of the F'Naar war clan standing in the Latharian hierarchy.

Fortunately for humanity, the K'Vass were about as large and powerful as Lathar clans got. They also had royal links up the wazoo and a sense of honor that appeared to be absent in some of the others. She dreaded to think what would have happened had the T'Laat discovered them first. It wouldn't have been pleasant.

They passed several corridor intersections. She studied and noted each. One seemed to lead to personal quarters, the second to what looked like engineering sections, but it was the third that interested Jane the most. She recognized a discolored patch of metal on one of the bulkheads that she'd marked on the way in. That way led to the shuttle bay, and there was a weapons locker nearby. Nice to know.

"Lord Ishaan is looking forward to hearing about Earth, Lady Jane," Zaanar commented, motioning them ahead of him as they neared the end of the corridor. The double doors in front of them slid open at their approach. "He's been intrigued about your planet since we heard of your discovery."

She bet he was. He and every other horny warrior out there. Her lips compressed under the hood. They heard about a new planet and all they thought about was the possibility of getting their rocks off.

"Come in, come in. Welcome!" Ishaan rose as they entered the room, his leathers replaced by a loose silk suit that reminded her of old style martial arts uniforms in the dojos she'd hung around as a teenager. His dark hair was cropped short and his odd colored eyes, a muddy orange and green, glowed with anticipation. "Sit, please..."

"Thank you," Karryl murmured, seating her at the large circular table in the center of the room. It was loaded with covered dishes and platters of food. Most of them she recognized from the court. Looked like someone was out to impress. "Quite the spread,

F'Naar hospitality is indeed as generous as the stories say."

"I would like to think so. Please, dig in." Ishaan's smile was broad as he took a seat opposite but didn't reassure Jane one little bit. They might look good, and be utterly charming at times, but she wasn't fooled. All Lathar were dangerous as fuck. "So, Lady Jane. Where did you say you were from on Earth?"

I didn't. She suppressed her initial reaction. It was an interesting and not unexpected question. She doubted any of the Lathar were familiar with earth geography, but there was no reason to lie. "I was born just outside New London, in a secondary level complex."

"Ahhh. Sounds very pleasant." Ishaan nodded as though he had a clue where she meant.

"Indeed, but it pales in comparison to Lathar Prime," she replied, keeping her voice soft and sweet in her best impression of the perfectly submissive Latharian bond-mate.

Ishaan cut a glance at Karryl, then smiled. "I must say, brother, I am very impressed. I'd heard that earth females were difficult to manage and aggressive but you seemed to have trained your mate well in our ways. She seems as obedient as an Oonat."

At her side, she felt Karryl jerk slightly. His leg shook where it was pressed against hers, as though he was having trouble holding in his amusement. They both knew she was in no way, shape, or form subservient.

"I have been fortunate." Karryl reached for the goblet in front of him, turning the ornate vessel in one large hand. Ishaan's gaze flicked to it for an instant before returning to Jane.

"Some of the terran women are... well, let's just say they're more like men. Aggressive, warlike... deadly warriors who refuse to bow to any man." He leaned forward conspiratorially. "If you ask me, it's why their society is in such a shambles. Allowing their women such control..." He shrugged. "They need to feel the proper control of a man."

She was going to kill him. Like, *proper control* dead on the floor, kill him.

Karryl sat back, sliding her a little side look as he did with a little gleam in his eye. The bastard was baiting her on purpose. "I am, of course, lucky. Some human females are not like that. They know their place," he said and took a drink.

Ishaan nodded, triumph flaring in his eyes. "Then I am doubly fortunate. One, that you have such a well-trained mate and two, that you're stupid enough to drink from an unshared vessel."

Poison. Fear stalled Jane's heart as Karryl dropped the goblet. It bounced off the table, the contents spilling across the surface.

"No! Karryl!" She leaped to her feet, trying to get to him as he sat, his expression frozen. Hard arms wrapped around her from behind, Ishaan hauling her up against him to chuckle.

"Come now, my little terran beauty. Did you really think I'd let him keep you?" He pulled her hood clear, breath warm on the side of her neck. "You were mine the moment we rescued you on that planet. You just didn't know it yet."

"You make me sick," she hissed as Zanaar and another warrior yanked the immobile Karryl by his armpits out of the chair. "There is no honor in using poison."

"Honor?" Ishaan barked out a laugh. "Who cares about honor? I care about results. Take him below and space him," he ordered Zanaar.

"No! Leave him alone," Jane cried out, struggling against Ishaan but not too much. She had one shot at this, and she damn well better make sure she pulled it off, or they were both dead. "Karryl, help!"

"Shhh, shhh." Ishaan released his grip with one

hand to soothe her. "Your warrior can't save you, beautiful."

She went still, not sagging against him but centering herself. "You know something?"

"What?" he asked, sick eagerness in his voice as he crowded his front side to her back, hands starting to move over her body.

"I don't need any man to save me."

Lifting her knee, she stamped on his foot, then shoved her ass back hard into his groin. He grunted with pain, forced to bend at the waist to keep his hold on her. She slammed her head back and savored the crunch as the blow spread his nose over his face.

"You little *draanthic!*" he hissed, backing as she spun around, and wound his fist back to hit her.

She didn't give him the chance. Bursting into movement, she landed two solid jabs into his face, right into his broken nose. He howled in pain, stumbling away from her but there was no chance she was letting him go.

He swung wildly, but she ducked under the punch. Her movements explosive, she hammered a body shot into his ribcage, then followed it up by slamming her elbow into the side of his face. Stumbling, he tried to get a decent block into place but she was on a roll. Kicking out, she drove her foot into the side of his knee. He swore as the limb gave under him, sprawling to the ground.

Flipping faster than she'd expected, he pulled a knife from the sheath on his wrist. Adrenalin coursed through her, making everything brighter and louder. She kicked the blade away and pulled the blaster from her hip holster. This asshole had poisoned her man, so he was going to pay.

Ishaan froze, his gaze flicking from her to the muzzle of the blaster and back again. "You wouldn't... women don't have the—"

She pulled the trigger. The bolt slammed into his forehead, right between the eyes. Eyes that retained their look of surprise even as the light faded from them.

"Women don't have the balls?" she asked the body before her, eyebrow raised. "Mate, mine are cast fucking iron.

11

Fuck. Karryl swore mentally to himself as the two warriors carried him out of the room. Poison. Of all the low down, dishonorable... He should have expected something like this from Ishaan F'Naar. The man was no warrior, he was a *keelaas* snake.

"Goddess, he weighs a ton," one of the warriors carrying him complained, grunting with effort. No surprise there. Karryl wasn't the smallest of men, his body packed with muscle from years of combat. A body now rigid from the effects of the poison, and unwieldy to carry.

Travenis Root. He knew immediately what Ishaan had used. It was the only thing that would render a warrior incapable within seconds. Although a small dose wouldn't kill a man as large as him; the cold embrace of space would end his life just as sure as a larger dose would.

He had to get out of this, but how? He was on an enemy vessel, poisoned, and with no way out. The only advantage he had was that they didn't know Jane wasn't the meekly submissive woman they thought her to be. Or that she was armed.

His only regret was that he wouldn't be there to see their reaction.

Help, when it came, was from an unexpected quarter. The complainer grunted again, his grip slipping. Karryl snorted in his head. The male needed to spend more time in the training rooms if he couldn't carry an inert body.

"Let's get this piece of *draanth* to the airlock. Maybe when Ish is done boning the earth woman, he'll put in at *Zentan Four* and we can get some action. There's an oonat female in one of the brothels just begging for my dick."

The warrior on the other side let go suddenly. Karryl held his breath as he canted sideways, recognizing the unmistakable sound of a blaster gun sliding from its leather holster. His view changed to a pair of heavy combat boots.

"Not happening." The growled voice of the

second guard was deep and familiar—Zaanar's. The sound of a blaster shot was followed by the dull thud of a body hitting the deck.

"Asshole," Zaanar muttered, crouching next to Karryl. He pulled a med patch from his pocket, and ripping it open with his teeth, slapped it on the side of Karryl's neck.

The antidote surged instantly through his system and he took a ragged breath. Lurching to a sitting position he coughed violently, trying to expel the drug as quickly as possible.

"Sorry about that, friend," Zaanar murmured, clapping him on the back. "I didn't expect that piece of *draanth* to stoop to poison."

Karryl nodded, waving him away as he clambered to his feet. The fact this other man carried antidote patches sang volumes. That was the least of his worries. His body ached like he'd played chicken with a sub-light shuttle but he had more important things to think about than why the other warrior had helped him.

"Jane!" Tearing himself away, he raced back into the room, fear surging through him at what he'd find and stopped dead in the doorway.

The scene was not exactly as he'd expected. Jane stood over Ishaan's body, a pistol pointed at his head, and her robes open and billowing to reveal she wore a warrior's combat leathers. The pool of blood under Ishaan's head said she'd shot him point blank. The hard look on her face as she turned around said it was without mercy.

"*Goddess,*" Zaanar murmured behind him. "She's..."

"Mine," Karryl growled, striding forward to haul her into his arms. She didn't argue, embracing him fiercely.

"Shit, I thought you were dead," she murmured, face tucked against his neck. Pulling back, she looked him in the eye. "I was going to take this fucking place apart."

"So I see. I gather he upset you. Didn't like his submissive comment, eh?" Karryl looked over her shoulder at the dead warrior. The sight inspired no pity. He'd never liked the F'Naar and so far they'd proven his suspicion correct.

Her lips quirked. "Something like that, yes."

She stepped away, looking with interest at Zaanar. The warrior hadn't taken his eyes off her, utter reverence on his face. Karryl hid his smile. The earth females were beguiling, none more so than his Jane.

"And who's your little friend? I'm assuming he's the reason you didn't end up sucking cold space?"

"A very good question." He hadn't expected much in the way of hearts and flowers from his mate, but her pragmatism and the speed she reverted to warrior impressed even him. Turning, he studied Zaanar with a hard look. Sure, the male might have saved his life, but no Lathar did anything without an angle.

"Who are you? Because you're sure as *draanth* no F'Naar."

Zaanar opened his mouth to speak but Jane cut in, her eyes narrowing. "You're Xaandril's son, aren't you?"

The younger warrior gasped. "How the fuck did you know?"

Karryl swore as recognition hit. It was all there, all the clues. The hair that was slightly lighter at the sides where dye couldn't get a hold, the voice...hells, even the way he moved. He was the Champion's issue through and through.

Jane arched her eyebrow. "A child could see through your disguise. Looks like your lot could take lessons from humans on spying. We've been doing it to each other for millennia, with great success."

"Oh?" Zaanar seemed eager for any tidbit of information. "You are a spy?"

She laughed, checking her blaster before re-holstering it.

"Hell no, I'm a professional soldier, son. Live hard, die young, take out as many of the bastards as you can. Death or glory." She winked. "What's your name?"

"Xaandrynn..." He stood, feet shoulder width apart as he studied them carefully. Only an idiot would not have realized they were far more dangerous as a team than apart and that he was outgunned. "My friends call me Rynn."

The sound of booted feet and shouts in the corridor outside drew all their attention. Karryl snatched his blaster, palming a blade at the same time. The F'Naar were going to be pissed that their leader was dead, and just as determined to take a female as a prize for whichever warrior emerged triumphant as their new leader.

"Well, Rynn. Looks like we need a ride for three off this ship," he growled, moving to the side of the door, ready for action. "Shall we take a stroll down to the shuttle bay?"

THE FIGHT through the F'Naar ship was fast and furious. At first the two warriors tried to put themselves between Jane and the enemy but thanks to the sheer numbers they faced, that didn't last long.

Her world became a maelstrom of laser bolts and hand-to-hand combat as they ripped through the opposition like a ball of razor wire. Blaster in hand, she used it with surgical precision to cut a swathe through the F'Naar. They fell before her, and those who didn't, fell prey to Karryl's or Rynn's blades.

They reached the shuttle bay, fighting a fierce rear-guard action as another group of F'Naar followed.

"Get the engines started," Karryl bellowed at Rynn as he took up position by the side of the hallway door. "Jane, get this thing closed."

She scooted into cover as a volley of laser blasts peppered the air where she had been. One thing was sure, they might revere women but they sure as hell weren't bothered about killing her now battle was joined. Obviously a case of if they couldn't have her, no one could. Childish assholes.

Yanking the cover off the console, she looked in dismay at the control pad. Unlike the emperor's shuttle with its AI enhanced control panels, this was all lines and squiggles.

"This makes no sense," she yelled, ducking out of cover for a second to fire off a volley down the corridor. "You do it, I'll cover!"

He nodded, and things happened fast, too fast for her to stop them. As he launched himself out of cover to the other side of the door, a warrior ducked around a corner down the corridor with what looked like a grenade launcher on his shoulder.

"*Kaaaaarrrryyyllll!*" she yelled a warning, but it was too late. Time seemed to slow as the energy blast raced toward him. Throwing herself to the side, she tried to knock him out of the way but it was no good. It hit him in the shoulder and spun him. He slammed into the deck and lay motionless.

"*Nononono!*" she cried out, turning and firing at the door control panel. It exploded into a shower of sparks and the door slid shut on the warriors charging up the corridor. It wouldn't hold them long.

Heart racing with fear and adrenaline, she skidded to her knees next to her fallen warrior. Instantly, she knew it wasn't good. He looked terrible, his skin pale and the leather over his shoulder blackened and cracked. Blood and burned flesh visible through the gaps.

"Karryl? Talk to me," she ordered, shoving two fingers into the side of his neck. There was a pulse. Relief left her lightheaded for a second.

He groaned, eyes flickering open. "Jane? Go...you have to go. Get out of here."

"Without you? Not happening, handsome." Standing, she pulled him up. "Come on, soldier. We're hauling ass. We live or die *together*. You got that?"

"Yes, ma'am." He chuckled and clambered unsteadily to his feet, then coughed.

It was weak and blood traced a thin line from the corner of his lips. Shit, that didn't look good. She'd been on enough battlefields to know when a soldier was badly, *badly* injured. Panic hit her, wailing in the corner of her mind she banished it to.

"Good. As long as you realize who's in charge, we'll get along fine." Sliding under his arm, she ignored the muffled blasts and shouting behind the shuttle bay doors and headed toward the ship. It was the longest walk she'd ever taken. She took as much of Karryl's weight as she could, expecting the F'Naar to break through the door and shoot them in the back any second.

They didn't, nor did Karryl collapse as she'd

expected. He made it through the door before his legs gave out. They sprawled on the floor.

"We're in, punch it!" she ordered Rynn, but he was way ahead of her. The engines roared, lifting them even as the shuttle door slid shut, sealing them safely inside.

She looked down as Karryl coughed, struggling for breath.

"Don't you dare die on me, asshole. Or I'll bring you back just so I can kill you myself, you hear me?" she promised, but he'd already slipped into unconsciousness.

"Hold on," Rynn yelled over his shoulder. "This is going to be a rough ride."

Unable to do anything else, she covered her fallen man and held on for both of them.

THE JOURNEY back to Lathar Prime seemed like an eternity. Karryl didn't regain consciousness, his skin deadly pale and his pulse growing more sluggish by the hour. Rynn, more familiar with the Latharian medkit and its mobile single-body stasis unit, grew so silent that she had to look at him to reassure herself she wasn't alone.

Through it all, she sat by Karryl's side, stroking his hair back from his face until Rynn finally announced their approach to the Latharian home world. Now, less than an hour later, she felt even more useless as Laarn moved around a big diagnostic bed. Her unconscious warrior lay on it, still out for the count. He'd been stripped, his leather jacket cut from him to leave him naked to the waist, revealing the bloody and blackened mess of his shoulder.

The healer's face was grim as he studied the blue arc over Karryl. It showed a diagram of the warrior's body, red warning lines and lights all over it. A big scarlet area over his shoulder radiated lines outward, all reaching for his heart. More red surged through his veins, lights that represented his circulatory system flashing in warning.

As she watched, more and more alarms sounded. Laarn moved with the speed of a demon, altering settings and administering medication. Her hand stole up to her mouth. She didn't need to be medically trained to know Karryl was barely hanging on. Nor did she need to be psychic to realize that despite the fact they bickered all the time, Laarn really cared for his friend. It showed in his expression, in the tense set of his body as he fought to save Karryl's life.

He had to get better. He *would* get better, she told herself. Latharian technology was much more advanced than humanity's. What would kill a human was little more than a common cold for the Lathar. Surely?

Finally Laarn paused, gaze intent on the readouts as they stabilized. The red warnings had been flickering between red and amber. One by one, each turned to amber and held steady. She wrapped her arms around her waist, trying to hold her hope in check. She'd seen that look on the faces of medical staff before. It often preceded the words "don't get your hopes up."

The healer sighed and stepped back, shoving a loose strand of his hair behind his ear. Unlike most warriors she'd seen, he wore his long hair tied at the nape of his neck. Probably because of his job.

He turned to her, arms folded across his chest, and she swallowed. Laarn had always been the one warrior of the K'Vass she'd never been able to work out but his expression now made her shiver. It was cold. Dead.

"There's a lot of damage. He took a direct hit from a high yield energy weapon, which alone would be bad enough, but his system was also weakened by the Travenis Root..." He shook his head. "The next twelve hours will be critical as we drain the poison. *If* he survives that, we'll know more about what we're dealing with."

Tears welled in her eyes. Not bothering to hide them, she bit her lip. "Can...can I stay with him?"

"You *are* staying with him." Anger flared in Laarn's eyes, taking her by surprise. Grabbing her by the back of the neck, he shoved her toward the bed. "Look at his wrist. *Look* at it!"

She didn't cry out, even though the healer's grip was punishing. Instead, she reached out with shaking hands to remove the brace from Karryl's wrist. When the skin was revealed, she gasped and dropped the cuff.

Black marks wrapped his skin like vines. Mating marks.

"All he ever wanted was a mate. You. He wanted you, waited for years and knew as soon as he saw you on that fucking base. Sure, he's loud and a bit of an idiot, but he is my friend," Laarn hissed in her ear. "And I would die for him, I would take his place on that bed in a fucking heartbeat...so you, faithless female, will stay right here. *If* he wakes up, it will be to see the face of his mate, with his marks on his wrist, as least once before he dies. Do I make myself clear?"

He shoved her forward, letting go and she fell across the bed. She didn't bother standing, the pain rolling through her too intense. Catching her breath, she nodded. "I'll stay. I'll stay as long as it takes. Whatever he needs."

Heavy footsteps behind her announced Laarn's departure. Closing her eyes, she rested her forehead against Karryl's wrist. Her fingers entwined with his and she desperately hoped for him to squeeze back, but they were lax. Unresponsive.

"I'm so sorry, love. I should have been faster, stronger, should have gotten you out of the way of that blast."

Tears fell, hot and stinging, as hope died a painful death.

She loved him. Completely and utterly. The only man in the galaxy who was her perfect match, her perfect Mr. Right...and she'd pushed him away, again and again.

Now he was dying and there was nothing she could do about it. Death wasn't an enemy she could charge down with a pulse rifle in her hand, or throw a grenade at. It wasn't an opponent she could outwit or out-strategize.

"Please God, or anyone who's listening," she whispered, praying for the first time in her adult life and not caring if Laarn or the whole damn Latharian race could hear her. "I'll do anything, just spare him. Please, I can't live without him."

Turning her head, she placed a gentle kiss on the inside of his wrist. "I love you, Karryl. You hear me? You can, I know you can. I love you, I have since the first moment I saw you...I was just too stubborn to admit it. Please come back to me. Fight and come back to me."

Unable to hold the tears back any longer, she crawled onto the big diagnostic bed and lay next to him. If they only had one more night together, she was going to spend it as close to him as possible.

One night to last a lifetime. She would make it enough.

12

---

*J*ane's soft tears tore his heart out.

Medicated and drowsy, Karryl swam up through the layers of unconsciousness to find his little human mate nestled against his side. Nothing hurt, but the fuzziness in his head said he was doped up on painkillers. Not a bad thing. He remembered the F'Naar ship, being poisoned and the fight in the shuttle bay. No one in their right mind would ever forget being hit with an energy blast; the blinding light and all-consuming agony would be etched into his memory as long as he lived. So would the fact his mate fought for him. Had carried him to safety and shielded him with her own body.

But all that paled into insignificance under two facts:

He had his mating marks.

Jane loved him.

Emotion and relief rolled through him. After all they'd been through, she loved him. Finally, everything was going to be okay.

She was nestled under his arm, against his side, her tears hot against his shoulder. Pulling her tighter, he rubbed her back gently. Her soft murmur was muffled against his side and her silent sobs deepened. Misery and pain filled the tiny sounds she made. The grief of such a strong woman brought so low brought him pain.

She shouldn't be crying over him. He needed to make things right, protect her. Make her smile and laugh. Love her as he had from the moment he'd seen her.

"Shhhh, my love," he whispered, pulling out of the sedative enough to lift his other hand and stroke her hair back from her face. "I'm not going anywhere. Not yet anyway."

"Karryl?" she lifted her head to look into his face, hope warring with pain as though she couldn't believe what she was seeing and hoped, but dared not to, at the same time.

"You're awake! Oh my god, how are you feeling?" She scrambled to a sitting position, pushing his hair back from his face.

"Laarn! He's awake! Karryl's awake," she yelled, trying to slide from the bed to get the healer, but Karryl stopped her with a hard grip on her arm.

"No, stay with me. We're bonded, it helps to hold you close."

He flicked a glance down to the dark marks around his wrist, tired triumph filling his body. She was his mate in every way that mattered. The other half of his soul made just for him.

"Laarn will know I'm awake. The diagnostic program will alert him."

And if the pain in the ass healer thought he was moving Jane, then Karryl would just have to hand him his ass on a plate. No one was moving his mate now that he'd gotten her into his arms. No way, no how.

"Are you sure I'm not hurting you?" Concern was written on her face as she lowered herself tentatively into his embrace. He shook his head, closing his eyes for a moment to savor touching her.

"No. I think Laarn hit me up with enough painkillers to drop a *penachia.*" He chuckled, knowing she wouldn't have a clue what one was, and the thought striking him as highly amusing. They were so different—born on different planets, from different races—who knew they'd find perfection in each other? "Not enough to mess with my hearing though...and I recall a certain female telling this male she lo—"

"Loves you," she interrupted, rising on her elbow to look down at him. Her odd-colored eyes were steady and honest as she held his gaze. If he'd thought she'd act coy and verbally dance around the subject, he was wrong. Like the soldier she was, she went right for the bull's eye.

"You heard right. I love you. You're stubborn and a pain in the ass, and luckily damned hard to kill, but I love you." Leaning forward, she brushed her lips over his. "And if you're still serious about your claim over me, then I accept."

Emotion and love exploded through Karryl, warming his body from his chest out, and he slid his hand up her back into her hair. Slowly, he drew her down to kiss her softly, then not so softly.

"I've always been serious about claiming you as mine," he broke the kiss to whisper. "The moment I saw you, that was it. We didn't know humans had women, let alone fierce warrior women. I'd always thought I wanted a meek, biddable little mate to ease my body at the end of a hard day..."

He chuckled as she made a noise and slapped his uninjured shoulder lightly.

"Turned out I didn't want that at all." He massaged the back of her neck lightly, delighting in how delicate, yet strong she was. "Turned out I wanted a stubborn little female who would argue with me at every turn and fight for my life with her own. Even if she did dump me on my ass in front of my brothers. Do you know how much *draanth* I got over that?"

"Hey! You asked for it. Never touch a soldier without her permission."

His thumb paused on the side of her neck and he tilted his head in question. "Do I have permission now?"

Her eyes warmed, still looking suspiciously wet, and she smiled softly. "Always, now and forever."

"Aren't humans supposed to wear white dresses or something to get married?" Laarn asked, standing next to Karryl as they watched the human women crowd around Jane.

It had been a week since he'd left the medbay, fully healed. The only reason they'd waited this long was because Jane insisted the divorce papers from her previous marriage and her resignation from the Terran military were delivered to Earth before they'd married.

Their bonding ceremony had been short and sweet. No grand hall and crowds like Tarrick and Cat's, just a simple exchange of words in the garden of Karryl's home surrounded by their closest friends. The sun was low in the sky, lending a golden glow to the scene as they'd pledged their love beneath a canopy of herris blossom and under the eye of the emperor himself.

A fond smile creased the big warrior's lips as he watched his newly-bonded mate...or bride, as he should call her since she was human. Sliding a sideways glance at the healer, who had surprised him by offering to act as second at the ceremony, he asked. "I believe so, but do *you* want to tell her that?"

Like him, Jane had opted for black leather for the ceremony, although she'd relaxed enough to let the other women thread tiny flowers through her short hair. In her hands, she carried a bouquet of wildflowers, their chaotic beauty a perfect match for his unpredictable mate. He didn't care that the outfit was unconventional, from neither of their cultures. Somehow it combined both and was absolutely, uniquely, Jane.

"Hell no," Laarn snorted, folding his arms, his feet shoulder width apart as he watched the women. His gaze seemed to light on the slender figure of Jess, Cat's quieter friend, rather a lot, but Karryl chose not to mention it. "Do I look suicidal to you?"

"Maybe not. But you are a ruthless bastard." Karryl took a swallow from the tankard in his hand. "Letting Jane think I was at death's door was cruel."

Laarn shrugged, eyes narrowed. His expression, as usual, was difficult to read. Of the two brothers, he was the more inscrutable. "Maybe. But effective. I figured she was just as pig-headed as you and needed the push. Would you rather I hadn't?"

"Hells, no." His gaze tracked his bride as she spoke with the emperor.

Daaynal, as always, was impressive and charismatic. Like most of the warriors present, he wore combat leathers. A lesser man would have felt inadequate, but Karryl had no fears that even a throne would turn his mate's head.

She was very much her own woman and knew what she wanted. Fortunately, that was him. She lifted her head to catch him watching her and her smile heated his blood from his toes up.

"No, I appreciate all the help I can get. Human females are damn hard to work out at times."

Laarn's gaze cut again to the little human female next to Cat. She was quiet, absently rubbing her stomach as she listened to Tarrick and Rynn talk. A little devil prompted Karryl.

"Looks like Xaandril's son is popular with the Earth women. Who do you think will catch his interest, Kenna or Jess?"

Laarn didn't say anything, his body stiffened for a second before he shrugged nonchalantly. "One or the other. Perhaps Kenna, she seems more talkative."

"Yeah... probably." Kaaryl hid his smile. He had his answer. The healer was sweet on Jess. "So, would you really have taken my place on the bed and died instead of me?"

Laarn arched his eyebrow, accepting a tankard from one of the circulating waitstaff. "And gotten myself a woman? Hell, yes. To save your ugly ass? I'd have to think about th—"

"Heads up!"

Jane's call cut him off mid-sentence and her bouquet sailed through the air, landing smack-bang in the center of Laarn's chest. He caught it neatly with one hand, confusion written over his features. A second later the two of them were surrounded by laughing women.

"Errr, this is yours?" he held it out to Jane, who shook her head, her eyes alight with mischief.

"Not anymore. They're yours now. Human custom."

Karryl couldn't help a grin at his friend's confusion and reached for his mate. She settled against his side happily, her hand splayed over his chest possessively. "And...according to human custom, catching the bouquet means you'll be married next."

"Not. Happening." Laarn's expression darkened and he held the flowers at arm's length as though they were dangerous.

"Here," he shoved the bouquet at Jess, to the delight of the other women. She blushed, trying to refuse them. "You have them. I give them to you. You can get married next, not me."

"I don't think it works like that, brother." Karryl bent and scooped Jane into his arms, hefting her easily despite her squeal of protest. "Now, if you'll excuse us, I have a mate to claim."

～

THEY WERE MARRIED. Finally. And it was all without the pomp and ceremony of a typical human ceremony. Just two people promising to spend the rest of their lives together. Nestled comfortably in her new husband's arms, Jane smiled as he strode through the corridors of his childhood home.

Single story, its low ceilings and white plasterwork were rustic and a world away from the elegance of the palace but she didn't care. It was a family home and she could almost hear the echoes of a child's laughter. From the past or the future, she wasn't sure, but she could imagine the former and hope for the latter. Later though. Right now all her focus was on the man who carried her in his arms as though she weighed nothing.

"You planning on carrying me over the threshold?" she asked, winding her fingers through his hair, playing with the tiny braids. It was the threshold of his bedroom, but that counted, right?

He caught her gaze, his own darkening in a way that made her blood race. "I'm carrying you to bed, little female, where I plan to do wickedly delicious things to your body."

She grinned. "I like the sound of that. As long as I get to do the same to you."

He shouldered open the door to the master

bedroom and ducked inside. The room was dominated by a large bed, covered with blankets and furs. Candles were already lit, casting a soft glow around them.

Two steps took them to the edge of the bed and he stopped, looking directly into her eyes. His were clear and honest, so honest that she could see down to his soul. "You can do whatever you like, my love. But first, I'm going to prove to you which male you belong to...which male you'll always belong to."

"Oh yeah?" she arched her eyebrow as he slid her down the front of his body. Her breath caught. She felt every inch of his heavily carved muscles against her, the latent strength in his body as he held her, the power coiled within. "Do I know this male?"

He growled, crashed his lips over hers and kissed her like there was no tomorrow. Like this moment here and now was all they had, and all they'd ever have. He kissed her like he needed to commit every detail about her to memory. Heat and need crashed into her, over her, and consumed her. By the time he let her up for air, she was moaning and clutching at the front of his jacket.

"You might know him," he muttered, reaching for the zip down the front of her jacket and sliding it down. "He's the male whose heart you own. I love you, Jane. Don't you ever forget that."

"I won't. I love you, too," her admission was softly spoken but secure in the knowledge of his love for her.

He moved to shuck the jacket off her shoulders and she bit back her smile. She might have eschewed the traditional wedding dress in favor of black leather, but she hadn't forgone lingerie. No bride passed up the power of lingerie, even her. Especially delivered from earth, the silk and lace bra barely contained what little she had in the way of a bust, giving her a cleavage for once in her life.

"What sorcery is this?" he murmured, his expression reverent, one hand splayed around her waist as though he dare not touch.

"Well... I *am* female. Occasionally we like to wear lovely things."

His gaze collided with hers, the heat there enough to flay flesh from bones. She loved that look on his face. Loved knowing she'd put it there. That she could bring this powerful man to the edges of his control. "Things...implies plural. There's more?"

She barely finished her nod before he tumbled her to the bed behind them. Within seconds, her pants and boots were gone, leaving her clad only in the tiny thong. And a garter.

"What is this?" he asked, sliding the tip of his forefinger under the elastic.

"It's a garter. Human wedding tradition." Her explanation was breathy, catching with each brush of his fingers. She'd laughed when Cat had given it to her, but worn it as a bit of silliness. Right now, seeing the effect it had on him, she was glad she had. "You're supposed to remove it with your teeth."

"Really?" His face tightened and he slid down her body. "Who am I to deny tradition?"

Big hands smoothed up her thighs, holding her still as he bent his head. He ignored the garter in favor of placing gentle kisses on her thigh.

A murmur in the back of her throat, she let her legs fall apart, a blatant invitation for whatever he wanted. His sigh of pleasure whispered across her skin and he gripped the garter gently, dragging it down. Lifting her leg, she helped, a soft giggle escaping her throat. One that became a moan when he slid a big hand up the inside of her thigh.

"Any more human traditions I should know about?" he asked lightly, deceptively.

She shook her head. "None I can think of unless you count the—" She gasped as he pushed her thong to the side and stroked his fingers through her folds. "Ohmygod, yes that..."

"Good, because now I have a few traditions to follow." His grin was wickedness personified as he moved closer to claim her lips, his fingers stroking a sensual pattern over her needy clit. Within seconds, he growled at the barrier of her panties and tore them from her. The bra followed, thrown heedlessly to land somewhere on the floor behind them.

Her moan was visceral and lost under his lips. She eagerly took everything he had to give and more. Not a shred of embarrassment rolled through her as she rode his hand. Her hips rocked, urging him on. A message he obviously got loud and clear because he slid two fingers deep. Pumped them in the silken grip of her pussy to make her ready for him.

She whimpered, their kisses hot and open-mouthed. Drugging and addictive. He was a fire in her blood. A need she didn't want to be cured of. It didn't matter how many times they did this, it was always as explosive as the first time. More so. Like their need and passion for each other increased each and every time.

Reaching down, she grabbed his wrist. "Now, please. No teasing. I need you."

He pulled back and searched her eyes. The tightness of the control he exerted over himself was written on his face.

"Are you sure? I don't want to hurt you..."

"You won't. Do it. Now."

He nodded, his hair falling forward to frame his face. His knee thrust between hers and he moved over her. Settling himself between her thighs, she sighed with pleasure as the head of his cock brushed against her. Hot, hard, slick with precum, she parted her legs wider in invitation.

He dipped his hips, gripping his cock to fit the head against her properly. He bit his lower lip, the look on his face so sexy, she caught her breath, and surged forward. Claiming her and mating them one in a single, smooth thrust.

"Ohhhhh..." she moaned as he filled her. Her body tensed, pussy throbbing and pulsing around his invasion. "That feels so good."

"Yeah?" He slid his arm under her shoulders, his hand cupping the back of her neck to hold her still, altering her position to where he wanted her. "Then you'd better hold on, little human, because it's about to feel a hell of a lot better."

And he set about proving his statement, for the rest of the night and a promise for the rest of their lives. Claiming her, just as she'd claimed him, her alien warrior.

Thank you so much for reading CLAIMING HER ALIEN WARRIOR!

I hope you loved meeting Jane and Karryl. The next book in the Warriors of the Lathar Series is **PREGNANT BY THE ALIEN HEALER.**

What happens when you mix a warrior surgeon determined to save his people and the human woman he can't live without?

Get PREGNANT BY THE ALIEN HEALER now! (minacarter.com/book/pregnant-by-the-alien-healer)

I appreciate your help in spreading the word, including telling friends. Reviews help readers find new books! Please leave a review on your favorite book site!

SIGN UP TO MY NEWSLETTER! https://minacarter.com/newsletter/

MORE IN THE WARRIORS OF THE LATHAR SERIES…

Adored by the Alien Assassin

She's a nurse, not a spaceship pilot. And why are aliens so damned hot?

Nurse Jac's life is boring. It certainly doesn't include aliens, unless they're on TV. But then the shit hits the fan and she finds herself on an alien ship with her charge frozen into a giant blue ice cube.

What's a girl to do? Kiss the hot alien, then knock him out of course. The problem is, she can't drive a car, never mind fly an alien spaceship. Which is a problem when hostile aliens board the ship…

Go to earth. Find a woman. Bring her back. Simple.

Rynn is an assassin. Normally. Now it seems he's a delivery boy. Sent to earth to retrieve a sick female, he's anticipating an easy trip. If he spends a little time getting to know the local culture… well, that's just a perk of the job. Right?Human females are fascinating, especially Jac, the sick female's nurse. He'd thought the warriors who'd fallen for humans had defective genes. But Jac is something else. Tiny. Delicate. Beautiful. HIS.

When an attack puts them in danger, he escapes earth with not one, but two human females in his care. What could possibly go wrong? Apparently... everything.

GET YOUR COPY NOW!

(minacarter.com/book/adored-by-the-alien-assassin)

Check out the rest of the series!

(minacarter.com/series/warriors-of-the-lathar)

ABOUT THE AUTHOR

Mina Carter is a *New York Times & USA Today* bestselling author of romance in many genres. She lives in the UK with her husband, daughter, a tank of a Staffordshire Bull Terrier, and a bossy cat.

Connect with Mina online at:
minacarter.com

facebook.com/minacarterauthor
instagram.com/minacarter77
bookbub.com/profile/mina-carter

Printed in Dunstable, United Kingdom

65112549R00121